SPARKS FLY WITH MR MAYOR

BY
TERESA CARPENTER

DID YOU PURCHASE THIS BOOK WITHOUT A COVER?

If you did, you should be aware it is **stolen property** as it was reported *unsold and destroyed* by a retailer. Neither the author nor the publisher has received any payment for this book.

All the characters in this book have no existence outside the imagination of the author, and have no relation whatsoever to anyone bearing the same name or names. They are not even distantly inspired by any individual known or unknown to the author, and all the incidents are pure invention.

All Rights Reserved including the right of reproduction in whole or in part in any form. This edition is published by arrangement with Harlequin Enterprises II BV/S.à.r.l. The text of this publication or any part thereof may not be reproduced or transmitted in any form or by any means, electronic or mechanical, including photocopying, recording, storage in an information retrieval system, or otherwise, without the written permission of the publisher.

This book is sold subject to the condition that it shall not, by way of trade or otherwise, be lent, resold, hired out or otherwise circulated without the prior consent of the publisher in any form of binding or cover other than that in which it is published and without a similar condition including this condition being imposed on the subsequent purchaser.

® and TM are trademarks owned and used by the trademark owner and/or its licensee. Trademarks marked with ® are registered with the United Kingdom Patent Office and/or the Office for Harmonisation in the Internal Market and in other countries.

First published in Great Britain 2010
Harlequin Mills & Boon Limited,
Eton House, 18-24 Paradise Road, Richmond, Surrey TW9 1SR

© Teresa Carpenter 2010

ISBN: 978 0 263 87690 1

Harlequin Mills & Boon policy is to use papers that are natural, renewable and recyclable products and made from wood grown in sustainable forests. The logging and manufacturing process conform to the legal environmental regulations of the country of origin.

Printed and bound in Spain
by Litografia Rosés, S.A., Barcelona

Dear Reader

Sometimes an author is lucky, and a character comes along who truly charms her. Cole Sullivan was just such a charmer for me. He truly believes his 'love them and kiss them goodbye' attitude is a noble endeavour. If there are no strings, there are no hurt feelings when the time comes to move on. And he's just charismatic enough to pull it off and still remain friends with the ladies in his life.

He meets his match in a young widow, with commitment issues of her own and a toddler precocious beyond her years. Family connections toss Cole and Dani together, while city politics pit them on opposing sides of a community issue. For all their efforts to dodge each other, life soon sets them up for a fall—straight into love.

I wish you joy in their story.

Teresa Carpenter

For Mike and Christy.
This book would never have gotten finished
without your help this last year.
And for Mom and Kathy for their patience, support, and love.

CHAPTER ONE

"I'M GOING to marry Cole when I grow up," a small voice said from the backseat.

"You are?" Dani Wilder glanced at her three-year-old daughter in the rearview mirror. Her mahogany curls were the perfect blend of her father's dark chocolate hair and Dani's burnished copper tresses. Fate had blessed her daughter with her daddy's deep blue eyes since Dani's were a nondescript gray. Faith met Dani's gaze and grinned.

"Yep." She confirmed her wedding plans. Never one to sit still, she kicked her black patent leather shoes against the seat back. "He says I'm his number-one sweetheart."

Dani gritted her teeth and determined to talk to Mr. Cole Sullivan at her earliest opportunity. A picture of the man came to mind, ruggedly handsome with mink-dark hair and brilliant blue eyes. He was tall and broad, with the lanky build of a runner.

They'd moved to Paradise Pines ten months ago, and she hadn't been in town for more than a week before learning of the mayor's reputation with the ladies. A total charmer, he was the love-'em-and-leave-'em type. Which said it all as far as she was concerned. It hardly mattered that he mysteriously stayed friendly with his castoffs. She wasn't letting the man mess with her little girl's head.

She made a left-hand turn into the restaurant parking lot and looked for a park. They were on the way to dinner with Samantha Sullivan, Dani's best friend since high school, and her family.

Samantha was the reason Dani chose Paradise Pines when she decided to move to a smaller, safer town to raise Faith.

"Don't you think you should have asked me before agreeing to marry anyone?"

"When I grow up, I'll be a big girl. But I'll still ask you, Mommy."

Dani smiled as she pulled her hybrid car into a spot near the front door. She was lucky to have such an agreeable child. She turned in her seat and straightened the hem of Faith's pretty pink dress. The outfit had a short jacket to match; the two pieces were piped in black and two heart-shaped black buttons decorated the jacket.

"You sure look pretty tonight."

Pleased, Faith patted her skirt. "You look pretty, too, Mommy."

"Thank you. Remember, you're going to be good tonight. Mind your manners and behave yourself."

Faith nodded and Dani got out to walk around and release the little girl from her seat.

"Do you think Cole would be my daddy instead of getting married? Then he could live with us, and I don't have to wait until I get bigger."

Pain stabbed Dani in the heart, which made her mad for not anticipating the question. Faith's newest and dearest desire was for a daddy.

Dani longed to tell Faith she had a daddy, but though Dani often shared pictures and stories of her father with Faith, the reality was he'd never be real for his daughter.

She wanted someone to play with, to look up to, to tuck her in at night.

"It's not that easy, Sweet Pea." Especially not with Cole Sullivan, who by all appearances was allergic to any form of commitment. He probably took two seconds to make a decision and never suffered any doubts.

"Why not?" Faith took Dani's hand as they walked toward the large wooden doors of the steakhouse.

"Because a daddy is part of a family. You and me, we're our own family."

"But we could ask Cole to be part of our family."

Or not.

"It doesn't work that way. Mommies and daddies are supposed to love each other, and I don't really know Mr. Sullivan." Which was true. Though she'd seen him on several occasions in his capacity as mayor, socially she'd only been in his company three times and always in a group setting. Every time she'd kept her distance.

He was Samantha's brother-in-law. Faith knew him because Samantha babysat for Dani in the afternoons three times a week. She understood Cole enjoyed playing with the kids and was a frequent visitor to the house.

"Oh." Totally despondent, Faith sighed her disappointment.

Little drama queen. Dani loved her to pieces.

As she reached for the door handle, boots sounded on the wooden porch behind them.

"There's my favorite girl," a deep voice said as a muscular arm reached around Dani to grab the door and hold it open.

Startled, she looked up into smiling blue eyes.

"Cole!" Faith launched herself at the man's long legs. "What are you doing here?"

Good question. Dani could only hope he wasn't a part of their party. She bit back a protest when he hiked Faith up into his arms. Her little girl beamed down at Dani.

"Look, Mama, I'm bigger than you."

"Yes, I see." She lowered her gaze from her daughter to Cole Sullivan. "Mayor. Can you please put her down? You're wrinkling her dress."

He lifted one dark eyebrow, making Dani feel that she'd overreacted. But he didn't challenge her.

"It's okay, Mommy." Faith was the one to protest. She showed her preference by looping her tiny arms around Sullivan's neck.

"No, your mother is right, we don't want to muss this beautiful dress." He carefully set Faith on her feet. "There you go."

He returned his amused gaze to Dani. "No need to be so formal. You can call me Cole."

Was he laughing at her? What nerve. She had every right to protect her daughter as she saw fit.

"When you have a few minutes, I'd like to speak with you privately."

The smile slowly disappeared; he gave a noncommittal nod. "Sure. The Sullivan party," he said to the hovering hostess.

The teenager, dressed in unrelieved black, walked to her podium to check her list. Just then the big wooden doors opened and Sullivans spilled into the restaurant lobby.

Chaos ensued while greetings were exchanged. The brothers shook hands; of the same height and coloring, they had different builds. Where Cole was lean and ripped, Alex had more brawn. He easily handled the carrier with his seven-month-old son tucked inside.

Dani knew there were six Sullivan brothers altogether. The four she'd met were incredibly beautiful men, strong and male with dark hair and blue eyes. She had no doubt the twins, whom she hadn't met, were made from the same mold.

She was under no illusion that Samantha was hoping she'd hook up with one of them. But Dani just wanted to raise her daughter and build her business. Her gaze rolled over Cole Sullivan—she really didn't have time for a man in her life.

Samantha held the couple's two-year-old while their four-year-old ran forward to hug Faith. Samantha stepped up for her own hug and little Seth made the jump from her arms to Dani's.

"Hello, sweetheart." Dani kissed him on the head and smiled at her friend. "I'm glad we could do this."

"Me, too." Samantha hooked her arm around Dani's elbow. "We're going to have fun. Do they have our table ready?"

The hostess stepped forward. "Right this way."

Once they reached the table and the kids were settled into their seats, Cole stopped Dani from sitting down. His hand, warm and sure, cupped her elbow and drew her away from the group.

"Excuse us for a few minutes. We're going to have a small talk on the porch."

"We didn't have to do this now," she protested as he led her toward the exit. "After dinner would have been fine."

"No." He released her once they stepped outside. "I find it's best to address these issues early in the evening, then there's no opportunity for false expectations to grow."

"False expectations?" she repeated. What was he talking about?

He sat down on a bench deep in the corner of the porch and gestured for her to join him. She sat, found herself way too close to him and tried to scoot away, which almost sent her toppling to the ground. She reached out to save herself and ended up grabbing his leg.

Before she could snatch it away, he lifted her hand and patted it.

Mortified, she looked up to apologize and encountered kind blue eyes.

"You're a beautiful woman, Dani," he said in the gentlest of tones, "and I'm sure you're intelligent and witty and have a lot to offer a man. But you're just not my type."

She blinked as she processed his nice-guy routine. "You think I wanted you to ask me out?"

"There's no need to be embarrassed—"

"I'm not embarrassed. I'm annoyed." She pulled her hand from his. "I know I'm not your type, obviously I'm too old. You like them younger, a lot younger."

His eyes narrowed and his posture became defensive. "What are you talking about?"

"I'm talking about the wedding plans my daughter was making on the way over here tonight. Are you insane, making a comment like that to an impressionable three-year-old?"

"Ah." Comprehension dawned. "I thought a fictitious engagement would distract her from what she really wants, which is a daddy."

The breath caught in the back of Dani's throat. "Did she say that to you?"

He shrugged. "It was headed that way."

"I talk to her about her father all the time."

"Yes." His tone turned gentle again. "His name was Kevin, he went to heaven, and you miss him very much."

Dani's heart constricted, in sorrow for the husband she'd lost and in heartbreak for the daughter who sought to replace him in her life.

"He's not real for her." She thought

again, only realizing she'd spoken aloud when he answered.

"No. Someday she'll appreciate knowing him through you, but that day is far in the future."

"You sound as if you know."

"I lost my parents when I was ten. I remember them, but my grandfather I only know through my grandmother's memories. I'm told I take after him."

She felt for the little boy he'd been, but she couldn't let sympathy distract her. "I'm sorry for your loss. And I recognize your efforts to waylay Faith's absorption with you, but as you are neither daddy nor husband material, I'd appreciate it if you keep your distance from her." Expecting that to end the matter, Dani stood and dusted off her backside, ready to head inside.

"I can't promise to do that."

"Excuse me?" Shocked by his refusal, she turned back to him.

"Look, I'll do my best to stay away from Faith, but for the most part I only see her when I visit my nephews. I'm not going to avoid them, so I can't promise to completely avoid Faith."

"I'm her mother, you have to honor my request."

"Can you tell me positively that making myself scarce will change anything?"

"She'll lose her fascination with you."

"If I disappear from her life, she'll just transfer her desire for a daddy to someone else."

"There is no one else."

"There's no one else in your life. Faith gets out more."

A sad but true fact. And wasn't he less than a gentleman to point it out.

"Look, I'd never do anything to hurt your baby. She's a cute kid, clever and bright as a rainbow. I enjoy her company and I'm her friend. I'll try to visit the boys on days she's not there. And I won't encourage her, but I'm not going to ignore her. That would hurt her feelings."

Dani wanted to protest, to make him bow to her parental demand. But on a more rational level she knew he was right. He'd conceded to the spirit of her request and, much as she'd like to blame him, the root of the problem was with Faith, not him.

"We should head back in before someone

comes looking for us." He gestured for her to lead the way. "I don't know about you, but I'm hungry."

Dani wanted to pout but that would only upset Samantha, so instead Dani pasted on a smile and determined to have a good time. It didn't take long to see the man was surprisingly amusing and amazingly good with the children, which only made her feel foolish.

She drew in a deep breath, let it out slowly and decided being upset hurt her more than him, and she didn't want to give him the satisfaction of ruining her evening.

So she breathed in, breathed out then turned to Samantha with a witty anecdote of Mrs. Day coming in requesting a shampoo and comb-out for her miniature poodle, Pebbles.

Samantha laughed. "So how did you convince her you couldn't do it?"

"I didn't. Lydia from the sheriff's office came in, took one look at Pebbles, and pulled out a ticket book and began to write Mrs. Day up for health and safety violations. Mrs. Day couldn't get Pebbles out of there fast enough."

"That is so funny." Samantha shook her

head. "You know Lydia can't write tickets. She's administrative support."

Dani blinked at Samantha before grinning. "I didn't know. And thankfully neither did Mrs. Day."

"My grandmother raves about your salon, Dani," Alex said. "Says you make her look young and hip."

"Gram is young and hip," Cole put in.

"She's certainly young at heart." Dani could almost like him for that comment. Their grandmother, town matriarch Matilda Sullivan, was sharp as a tack with the energy and agility of a woman twenty years younger. "I admire her a lot."

"Be careful," Alex issued a good-natured warning. "I love her dearly, but she's not happy unless she's got her fingers in someone's life."

Yeah, and her current project was to find a woman to run against Cole for mayor in the upcoming election. They were on opposite sides of the current conflict in Paradise Pines on what to do with an endowment of land and funds for a community improvement project. Most of the men wanted a sports complex, most of the women a museum and botanical garden.

"I'll take that chance. Your grandmother has been very supportive in helping me get my salon up and going."

Cole focused his blue gaze on Dani. "That's because What A Woman Wants has become the hub for the group opposing the sports complex. She's using your shop to gather support for her newest pet project."

"The endowment is a hot topic of discussion at many of the businesses on Main Street." Dani's chin went up as if he were attacking her full-service salon and miniboutique. "I don't censor what my clients talk about as long as they pay for the services."

"Well, aren't you the entrepreneur?"

"What's an ontriprenear?" Faith looked a long way up to ask Cole. "What's an endowment?"

"It means your mom is a smart businesswoman. And an endowment means someone who used to live here donated a lot of money for the town to use for community improvement," Samantha answered Faith, and then she sent a narrow-eyed glare around the table. "And that's the end of that topic."

"Is it time for dessert?" Four-year-old Gabe wanted to know.

"Yes," his father confirmed and waved over the waitress. After all the orders were in, Alex reached in front of the high chair to take his wife's hand. "And now it's time for us to get to our purpose for this get-together. Samantha."

"Yes." Samantha beamed at Dani and Cole. "You are two of our favorite people, and we'd be so excited if you'd be Jake's godparents."

Both thrilled and appalled, Dani glanced from her friend's glowing face to Cole's only to find her nemesis looking oddly vulnerable.

"Are you sure you wouldn't rather have Brock or Ford?" he asked, referring to two of his brothers who were married with kids.

Samantha reached her hand out toward Cole, but it was Alex who answered. "We want you."

"Jake just loves you," Samantha added. "Nobody else can make him laugh like you do."

"Then I'd be honored." Cole stood to shake his brother's hand.

Dani saw Cole meant what he said. He'd been surprised by the request, and touched. Maybe it wouldn't be complete hell if they ever had to act as guardians in the future. Not that a godparent was expected to take on such responsibilities in today's age, but Dani would.

In a heartbeat. This was one decision she didn't need to worry over or second-guess, one result she'd honor with pride.

She'd take all the kids rather than let them get split up. Samantha meant that much to her. She'd been there at the worst point of Dani's life. And Dani loved the boys.

Samantha was looking at her with tear-bright eyes. "Dani?"

"Of course," Dani answered as tears stung the back of her eyes. "I'm flattered you would ask me."

"You're the sister of my heart. There's no one I would trust my child to more," Samantha said.

She stood at the same time Dani did and they laughed as they met in the middle for a huge hug.

"I feel the same," Dani assured her. "You can count on me."

"I always have. I'm so glad you're here in Paradise Pines now. The Sullivans are wonderful. They've embraced me and welcomed me into their extensive fold. But you and Faith are my family."

Dani's throat closed as tears threatened to spill. She had grown up in foster care. Decent homes for the most part, but always somewhat impersonal. Except for the short time she'd had with Kevin, she couldn't remember what it felt like to be part of a family. She didn't know what it meant to have a sister, but she figured Samantha came close.

"I'm glad to be here, too. This was a good move for us. Faith loves the boys." Wanting to lighten the mood, she leaned close and told Sam, "On the way here, Faith told me she's going to marry Cole when she grows up."

Samantha grinned. "He is a charmer, and she is a fan of his." She bumped Dani's shoulder. "Her mama should take note. Oh, here's the waiter with dessert. I ordered us both a double-fudge sundae with nuts. We're celebrating!"

She gave Dani one last hug before returning to her seat where she threw her arms around her husband's neck and gave him a big kiss.

Dani turned back to her chair to find Cole standing there ready to seat her.

Perfect. Playing nice for Samantha's sake, she allowed him to assist her. "Thank you."

"My pleasure." His warm breath tickled her ear as he bent over her. "It looks like I'm going to be daddy to your mama after all."

She sent him a quelling look over her shoulder. And he winked at her.

Oh, yeah, just perfect. Then she shrugged and reached for her spoon, ready to dig into double-chocolate fudge. Let him tease. Tonight was for celebrating.

CHAPTER TWO

"WE WANT YOU to run for mayor."

Dani removed the curlers from her client's hair one at a time, her attention more on the view reflected in her mirror than on the woman in her chair. Across the way, Cole Sullivan stood on the shallow steps of city hall talking to the owner of the hardware store and Dr. Wilcox, a chiropractor from the practice down the street.

Casual in blue jeans and a T-shirt, Cole stood several inches taller than the other two men as he listened intently to their discourse.

"Dani." The urgency in Matilda Sullivan's voice drew Dani's focus back to her shop. "Did you hear what I said? We want you to run for mayor."

"What?" Dani froze, her hand poised to

drop a curler into the bin beside her. "You were talking to me?"

"Yes, dear. We've decided you're perfect for the position."

"Oh, no. You're wrong. I know nothing about politics." It was all she could do to make sense of the propositions from election to election. "Isn't it too late to declare?"

"Tomorrow is the deadline. We've been talking this issue over for several weeks and I've noticed you listen more than you talk and when you do speak you're always the voice of reason. You're intelligent, calm and fair-minded. Paradise Pines couldn't do better."

"I don't know," Dani prevaricated, though it was a lie. Everything in her screamed *no*.

Matilda Sullivan continued. "We need a strong leader, someone the voters of Paradise Pines can sympathize with, someone with strength, resolve and determination. That's you, dear."

"Please say yes," Mrs. Day enthused. "As the widow of a hero, you'll make a very sympathetic candidate."

Dani blinked at the woman and then glanced at the women gathered around the room. All looked at her with varying levels of hope.

She shook her head. The woman Mrs. Sullivan described was exactly who they needed, but that wasn't Dani. Oh, God, since Kevin had died, she was afraid of everything. To pretend otherwise would make her nothing short of a fraud.

"I don't feel strong." It took all her willpower every day to get out of bed and put on a happy face for Faith. The need to provide for her daughter was what drove her to succeed at her business. Taking care of Faith and the shop took all her time, stole all her energy.

How could she possibly take on this challenge?

"You have more strength than you know. You're a single parent raising your little girl alone. You're making a success of this shop, no small feat in today's economy. Dani, a lot of people respect what you're doing."

"Thanks." While the sentiment made Dani feel good, she realized it obligated her, as well. Her success came at the expense of hard work, but also at the good will of the citizens of Paradise Pines. These ladies were regulars. Even the controversy itself had proved profitable for her as her shop was used more and more as gossip central.

If Dani refused to run for mayor, would disappointment in her cause business to slow? She didn't like to think her clients or friends were so shallow, but that only meant they wouldn't consciously dis her. Subconsciously they may decide to cut corners by doing a home pedicure, color, perm, etc. On the other hand, running for mayor meant a lot of publicity for her and her shop.

It was a lot to think about.

"Cole, we're only asking for one more term. We need you if we're going to win this endowment contest."

"You don't need me," Cole denied, seeing a full-time return to his nursery and landscape business slipping away. He really needed to get back to work. He missed his plants, missed getting his hands dirty. "The sports complex benefits more people and will generate more income. There's no question how the citizens of Paradise Pines will vote."

"The supporters of the museum project are vocal and well organized," Dr. Wilcox argued. "And your grandmother has a lot of influence. Only another Sullivan can sway the vote our way."

A highly visible, highly vocal member of the city council, Gram did wield a lot of sway over public opinion in the small town. "J.T. has declared. He's a good man."

"We need a Sullivan," Harold Palmer, owner of the hardware store, reiterated.

Cole glared across the street at the shop window for What A Woman Wants, the beauty salon his grandmother frequented, the store owned and operated by the lovely Dani Wilder. He hadn't been able to get her out of his mind.

"They don't even have a candidate. You have nothing to worry about."

"They will," Wilcox predicted. "My wife told me they were going to ask their chosen candidate today." He turned to face the street. "They've over at the beauty salon strategizing as we speak."

A bad feeling came over Cole. "Who's the candidate?"

"The new gal," Harold announced. "Dani Wilder."

Perfect, Cole thought. The thought of the two women in league together made Cole cringe. One was hard willed and manipulative and the other was a single parent driven to succeed, a dangerous combination. Hopefully Dani had the sense to turn his grandmother down. But after the way she'd rallied to Gram's defense, he didn't know if she'd have what it took to deny the persuasive old gal.

There had to be a way around this mess. Cole ground his teeth in frustration. The glass door in the next building over opened and the sheriff's office manager stepped out and strolled toward them.

"Lydia." He nodded and smiled at the approaching woman. Tall and thin limbed, she wore her black hair cropped close to her head while intelligence lit up lively blue eyes. She'd been with the sheriff's department for over thirty-seven years. As long as he'd been alive. She grinned and nodded back. "Mr. Mayor."

He shook his head at her formality, but she insisted it was a matter of respect. Just to tease, he winked at her before turning back to the businessmen waylaying him.

"What about J.T.?"

"Come on, Cole." Doc Wilcox shook his

head. "We need someone who knows how to handle women, and nobody knows women better than you."

Behind him, Lydia tripped over her own feet. Once she caught herself, she glared at the three of them, and then she made a smart one-eighty turn and headed across the street to What A Woman Wants.

Cole dropped his head to his chest. He should have said no sixteen months ago, then he wouldn't be in this position. He loved his hometown, the location, the people, the history, but he wanted his life back.

Still he sighed. "I'll think about it."

The men clapped him on the back then crossed the street to their respective businesses. Which of course drew Cole's eye to the new shop right in the middle on the opposite block. Lavender and aqua dressed the windows of What A Woman Wants, the colors suggesting a calm and soothing experience within. Or so his receptionist informed him as she raved about the new shop.

He wished he knew what was going on in there. Would Dani run for office? Sharp, stable, the widow of a hero, she definitely had weapons to bring to the table.

With Gram's support, the two women made a formidable combination, strong enough to beat a lesser opponent. He'd planned to step back this year. Truly, he didn't want to run for mayor again, but he'd do it to protect the best interests of Paradise Pines.

Running his hand over the back of his neck, he had the absent thought he needed to get a cut soon. His gaze sharpened on the shop across the way. Oh, yeah, he needed a cut, and he knew just where to get it.

The bell over the door jangled as Lydia stormed into the shop and set her purse on the counter with a thump. "Sign me up, girls, I'm a convert."

"Lydia, are you okay?" Dani stopped teasing on her updo to address the agitated woman.

"Steaming mad is what I am. I admit I was for the sports center. I've got grandkids. They like to play ball, and comfortable seats and a misting system sounded good to me."

"It's okay, Lydia. You're entitled to your opinion," Dani assured the woman.

"It's not that." Lydia gestured over her shoulder to where Cole stood talking to

Palmer and Wilcox. "They're over there hatching plans on how to *handle* us women, like we don't know how to make up our own minds."

"Oh, surely they didn't go there," Mrs. Day huffed.

"Oh, yes, they did." Lydia paced in front of the counter. She shook her head. "I expected better from Cole. He's usually smarter than that."

Dani rolled her eyes. Why was she not surprised by Cole's dismissive attitude? "That's my problem with this whole controversy. The sports complex jocks aren't even listening to our side. It's as if we're children and they have to protect us from ourselves. It's insulting."

Mrs. Sullivan placed a warm hand over Dani's. "You have the power to stop them."

Dani sighed and gave in to the inevitable. "I'll think about it."

When the door opened and closed again, all chatter abruptly ended. Cole Sullivan in all his masculine glory sauntered up to the counter. He sent a smile around the room, touching each woman individually.

Dani swore she heard a twitter and had to control an eye roll. Instead she pasted on her own anemic smile.

"Mayor," she said, "can I help you?"

"I'm here for a cut."

"Oh." She hadn't expected that. She glanced at the three occupied stations. "It'll be about twenty minutes before anyone's free. Would you like to come back?"

"I'll wait."

Dani tried to outlast Cole, hoping he'd get tired of the female chatter and peel away.

No such luck. And thirty minutes was all the proprietor in her would allow.

Her second hope, that the shop would empty out so there'd be less of an audience for the impromptu performance, was also doomed to failure.

Not only did nobody leave, new customers joined the crowd until her little shop nearly burst at the seams. The shop featured three hair stations, three pedi-massage chairs and two nail stations. Including her there were only four stylists, but no one seemed to mind. Every seat was occupied, plus two women wandered through the shop's miniboutique in the sizable lobby.

At least she'd profit from Cole's visit.

"Mr. Sullivan." She gestured for him to take a seat in her chair.

He sauntered over, tall and lean and graceful. Dani swallowed hard but held her ground.

Before he sat he leaned close. "Call me Cole."

"Sure." Her smile was all teeth. Not going to happen.

Determined to play this cool, as if he were any other customer, she fought an unnatural reluctance to touch him and fanned her fingers through his hair. For a good cut she needed to get a feel for the texture, curl and resiliency. Soft to the touch, his dark brown hair clung to her fingers as she combed the thick, healthy waves.

Sexy. And sweet sugar cookies, he smelled good, like clean earth and clean man.

"What do you want done today?" she asked.

Hearing the unusual huskiness in her voice, she gave herself a quick internal pep talk. *Pull it together, girl. You're a professional, he's a client, you can do this.*

"Same style, just shorter."

"Right." Picking up a spray bottle, she met his blue gaze in the mirror, careful to keep her demeanor cool and professional. "The cut comes with a shampoo or, if you prefer, I can just spritz you?"

"Oh, I want the whole experience." The words challenged even as his eyes glittered an invitation to enjoy the adventure.

"Of course." Dashed hopes were piling up. He wasn't going away and he wasn't going to make the visit easy. *Well, let's see how he likes the smock.* She used the garment instead of the cape because she felt it gave the shop a spa vibe.

Looking at the wide span of his shoulders, she grabbed an extra-extra-large from a lower drawer.

His eyes flashed as he donned the aqua robe, but he kept his comments to himself. She bit back a smile, wishing she'd had the guts to give him a lavender one. Yeah, let him embrace that adventure. But as always she played it safe.

"This way." She led him to the shampoo bowl behind a lattice screen.

"You have some good plants in here," he said. "The hydrangeas are nice. Did my grandmother bring them in?"

"Nice? They're gorgeous." Dani gestured

for him to sit. "She knows I love fresh flowers in the shop, so she brought them from her garden. They brighten the place up so much."

"Yeah, we had some good blooms this year." He sat and adjusted his length to fit the notched sink.

On the other side of the screen the chatter abruptly ended, though Dani doubted communication stopped. Instead it changed to whispers and low hisses as the women analyzed why he was here.

As she adjusted the water temperature and began to rinse Cole's hair, she felt the weight of his intense gaze. On his back, he really had nowhere else to look but at her. She was used to being in this position, but somehow his scrutiny unnerved her. Routine saved her. She added shampoo and began to massage his head.

Well, the good news was he'd soon smell like product instead of all male.

We? Her thought finally caught up with their conversation. Right, he owned a nursery; of course he'd help his grandmother with her yard. Dani squirmed, knowing she shouldn't begrudge him the compliment, but something about him scratched her wrong.

"Your rubber plant is looking sad, though. It probably needs to go outdoors."

The criticism stung, adding to the disturbing itch. "I've seen lots of them indoors, and I really like the look of it." She struggled for a moment between defensiveness and the health and well-being of her plant. Her love of plants won. "The corner it's in gets lots of sunlight, and I've tried some plant food. Is there anything else you'd suggest?"

He closed his eyes as she massaged her thumbs along the base of his skull. "Darn, that feels good. I may have to give up the barbershop for good." He sighed and then answered her question. "Outdoors is about more than just sunshine. It's also about lots of fresh air. The plant may be reacting to some of your products."

"I didn't think of that."

"It would probably do better in the lobby area, near a window or the door."

"Thanks, I appreciate the advice."

"No problem. It's pretty quiet," he said. "I thought this was supposed to be gossip central."

So he was putting it out in the open—he was here for information. How brazen, coming right into the enemy camp.

The garden talk had thrown her off for a few minutes, but he'd just been biding his time.

She leaned down and spoke directly into his ear. "You better want a haircut, because that's all you're going to get here."

He flicked her a glance. "Just don't scalp me and no one will be hurt."

"Don't make fun." She twisted the water off with more force than necessary. "These women feel safe here. I won't let you threaten that."

"Calm down, mama bear, your little cubs are safe from me. You're the one I'm here to see."

"Me?" Incredulous, she demanded, "Why? And couldn't it wait until Wednesday night? We're going to see each other at the christening class."

"It seemed like a good idea at the time."

He sat up and she swathed his head in a towel, lavender this time. Ha.

He went on, "I needed a cut and I heard the Gram squad was trying to talk you into running for mayor. One plus one and here I am."

She yanked the towel from his head. "How could you hear that when they only asked me twenty minutes ago?"

"Ouch." He rubbed his wet head. "Watch it or there won't be anything left to cut."

"Answer the question."

"I don't know." Standing, he shrugged dismissively. "Someone must have leaked the news. I hope you're not falling for their line."

"What? I'm not smart enough to run for mayor? I'm not savvy enough? What?"

"No." He began to backpedal. "I didn't say that."

"It's not a line. I'm honored they asked me to run. And you're not getting a haircut." She pointed toward the door. "Please leave."

"Wait. I didn't mean you couldn't manage the job."

"You can just stop. I won't be *handled*." As she spoke, she made her way back to her hair station. "But, thanks, you just helped me make up my mind. Get ready for a fight, because I will be running for mayor."

"Yeah!" The women broke into applause.

"Fine." Cole swept both hands through his damp hair and headed for the door.

"Oh, Mr. Mayor." She stopped him.

He half turned, hit her with a questioning glare. "Leave the robe."

CHAPTER THREE

"I can't believe I let him irk me into agreeing to run for office." Seated at the island counter in Samantha's kitchen, Dani rolled her coffee mug between her palms. "It makes me so mad at myself. I never jump into a situation without giving it careful thought. I wished you'd warned me what Matilda was planning."

"She never said anything to me." Samantha sliced a pound cake and transferred a piece to a plate for Dani. "Gram has her own way of doing things. She probably wanted to surprise you, give you less chance of coming back with preconceived excuses. She's devious like that."

"Well, it worked. I had no chance to formulate a response before Cole came in and got me all riled up. I swear, if they weren't on extreme opposites of this issue, I'd think they tag teamed me."

Samantha laughed. "That wouldn't be past them, but not this time. You're right, they're on separate sides." She clicked her coffee cup against Dani's. "I would have loved to see him in the lavender turban."

The memory tugged a smile out of Dani. "It was an impressive sight."

Samantha came around and sat down next to Dani, giving her a friendly shoulder bump. "You know, this might be a good thing. Since Kevin died, you've been a tad overcautious. You spend all your time with Faith or at the shop."

"I'm not that bad," Dani denied. She scowled. "I wish they wouldn't refer to Kevin as a hero."

Samantha cocked her head at the sudden change in topic.

"At the shop, Mrs. Day said I'd make a good candidate because I was the widow of a hero."

Samantha cringed, which was pretty much Dani's reaction. "Not our most tactful citizen, Mrs. Day," her friend sympathized. "But he did step between a bullet and a seventeen-year-old clerk in a holdup gone bad. That pretty much makes him a hero."

"I'm glad the girl wasn't hurt, but I'd rather have a live husband than a dead hero."

"Oh, sweetie, I know."

Dani accepted the comfort of a one-armed hug as an emotional lump clogged her throat. Kevin had been gone for two years, yet sometimes the grief felt so fresh. She swallowed hard as she fought for composure.

"I'm so glad to be in Paradise Pines and away from the city. I'll take a squabble about a million-dollar donation of funds over crime, drugs and violence any day."

"Amen to that." Samantha stole a bite of Dani's pound cake. "The endowment might cause a few arguments but there's not likely to be any bloodshed."

"Well, not if Cole stays out of my shop, anyway." Dani met Samantha's gaze and they both grinned.

Dani's resentment of Cole Sullivan resurfaced two days later as she sat behind him at the baptismal instruction class.

He'd baited her into declaring her candidacy when she usually preferred to weigh the situation carefully before making a decision. Not that any decision came easily these days.

At least she hadn't had time to brood, to decide one way and then the other, or to fret over how it would affect Faith, her business or the future.

There'd been no going back after making the announcement in front of the women in her shop. In order to build a successful business she needed to look strong and steady, not weak and foolish. So she was stuck.

Thanks to Cole Sullivan.

The only good news was she had no chance of winning. Just as the museum/garden proposal had little chance of winning. Winning? Ha, no one would even listen to them. That had become her goal, to get the predominately female supporters fair representation on the endowment issue.

She'd lose but the women would feel they got the respect of being heard, a win-win from Dani's point of view, and she'd get a little free promotion in the mix.

Which didn't let Sullivan off the hook.

His earnest absorption in the lesson did.

She held on to her snit for all of ten

minutes once the class started. Where many of the men in the room shifted restlessly, Cole paid close attention. Better than she did. He'd said he was honored to act as Jake's godfather and he obviously took the obligation seriously.

She admired his dedication enough that when he invited her for coffee afterward she agreed. A decision she regretted when she sat across from him in the diner.

This was way too intimate, just like when she'd had her hands in his hair at the shop.

"I can't stay long," she said, starting on her exit strategy. "I have to get home to Faith."

"How's my little fiancée doing?" he asked, mischief a devil in his blue eyes. "I do miss her."

She waited until after the waitress left water and coffee before shaking her finger at him. "That's not funny."

"It's a little funny."

"No, it's not." She shook her head, refusing to give into his charming smile.

"Come on, lighten up." He slid a hand across the table and traced a finger along the back of her wrist. "Wouldn't it be funny if we hooked up? What a story to tell the grandkids—I was engaged to your mom before I married your grandma."

She snatched her hand out of his reach. "Again, not funny. We are not going to hook up. Where do you come up with this stuff? I'm not your type, remember?"

She was still trying to convince herself that hadn't stung.

"I might have been too hasty." His intense gaze roamed over her hair, her face, her scooped-necked black shirt.

Heat bloomed within her. Something she hadn't felt in a long time. And had no business feeling now. Certainly not for this man. He was way out of her league.

Whatever. She shook off the unexpected, unwanted arousal.

"That was before you washed my hair. You give a great head message."

She gasped and quickly looked around. Thankfully, no one paid any attention. "You did not just say that in a public restaurant."

He lifted one dark eyebrow. "It's the truth."

"You're off your rocker. Never say that aloud again."

"Samantha wants us to hook up." He tried

looking hopeful when she knew, *knew*, he was pulling her chain. The man was a danger to women everywhere.

"She'll get over her disappointment."

"That's cold. Don't you care about your friend's feelings?"

"Not when it comes to my love life. Besides, Sami doesn't care which of Alex's brothers I hook up with—she just wants us to be sisters."

He laughed. "True. But I saw you first."

She shook her head at his nonsense. "Be careful," she warned him. "Or I may just take you seriously."

"There's hope for you yet, Wilder." He winked at her as he sipped his coffee.

Game over. She sighed and reached for the cream, able to breathe for the first time since sitting down. The way he riled her, the man was a walking adrenaline rush.

"So how is Faith?" he asked.

"Why?" Unprepared for the conversation to wrap back around to Faith, Dani's protective instincts kicked in.

"No why. She's a cute kid and I miss seeing her. I've been a good boy and done as you asked. I even missed seeing the boys yesterday, because I knew she'd be there."

Dani felt a bit of regret for the boys. She knew how crazy they were about their uncle Cole.

"I know. Sami told me you'd been calling ahead instead of just showing up. And I appreciate it. Faith misses you, too." She eyed him suspiciously. "Somehow she's figured out it's my fault and she's mad at me."

He held both hands up in a stop motion. "Don't look at me. As I just said, I haven't seen her."

"Yeah, as if that would stop you if you wanted to get a message through."

All levity left his expression. Obviously she'd hit a nerve, but she waved him off.

"I believe you. I'm just frustrated. Alex often goes home for lunch and spends time with the kids. He'd be a nice, safe fixation for her."

"But he's Gabe, Seth and Jake's daddy. She loves Alex, but she wants a daddy of her own."

And that's what hurt so much. But Dani knew he was right, his insight into her daughter was spot on. But short of marrying someone she didn't love, this was something she couldn't give to Faith. Unwilling to let Cole see how he got to her, she held his gaze, wishing the world were a different place.

"Be careful, Dani." The owner, a slim brunette with aqua eyes, set two pieces of banana-cream pie on the table and slid into the booth next to Cole. "You can't believe a word this guy says," Mattie Sullivan said. "It's all sweet talk and hot air with him."

Because she'd been staring him down, Dani caught Cole's flinch before he ramped up his customary humor and charm. "Dani, you've met my cousin?" he offered in the way of introductions.

She nodded.

"You need to watch it," he cautioned Mattie. "The lady and I are about to become parents together. I can't have her thinking bad things about me. I'm a sincere guy."

"Parents?" Mattie rolled the word out for maximum effect. "Congratulations. Wait until Gram hears. Get married and she may even let you back into her good graces."

"Godparents," Dani quickly corrected, with another frantic look around the room. She'd be lucky if she got out of here with her reputation intact. "Please don't encourage him," Dani said. "I've just got him off the topic of marriage."

"Really?" This time true surprise sounded

in the word. Mattie ran a questioning gaze over her cousin. "That doesn't sound like Cole. I've always thought he was allergic to the word."

"Go away—" he nudged the brunette with his shoulder "—you're cramping my style."

"Gram will be thrilled with this news." Ignoring him, she picked up his fork and took a bite of his pie.

"Hey," he protested, reaching for his fork. "That's mine."

His cousin held the utensil out of reach. "She may even forgive you for the whole sports complex debacle."

"Gram isn't going to forgive me for anything until I settle down and give her a real grandchild."

"Or three." She grinned and passed him the fork.

"Brat. Do me a favor and scram."

"Can't leave yet. I'm on a mission." She focused her blue stare on her cousin. "I want to cater the desserts for the Harvest Dance, but Sami plans to pick up pastry items from one of the big warehouse stores. Can you put in a good word for me?"

"Can't," Cole said. "You're family—I

can't show favoritism, it would be a conflict of interest."

"That's what Sami said. It's not fair I'm being penalized because I know the people in power."

"It's not fair to the community either," Dani said as she forked up a bite of pie. "Your desserts are wonderful."

Mattie smirked at Cole and then beamed at Dani. "Did I tell you how much I like you? You're too good for this big brute. Is it true you're running for mayor against him?"

After enjoying their playful banter, the question came as a cold slap. As levity clashed with harsh reality, panic raised its ugly head. That fast Dani felt overwhelmed by everything in her life. How could she take care of Faith and the shop and run for office, too? But what would happen to her reputation and her business if she let the ladies down? It was all too much.

A warm hand settled over hers, bring her back to the table, back to her senses. She followed the hand up a hair-dusted forearm, past a broad chest, over a relaxed mouth and landed in understanding blue eyes.

"Dani doesn't have to do anything she

doesn't want to do," Cole declared, sounding sincere, but was it truth or hot air?

Was he saying she could back out of the mayoral race without disappointing her new friends and clients? Or did he just want her to think she could so she'd leave the field clear for him?

Pulling her hand free, Dani confirmed her bid for candidacy and then quickly turned the conversation away from herself.

"So, Mattie, are you pro sports center or museum and botanical garden?"

Mattie glanced around the busy diner and shrugged. "These days I'm all about the food. But I grew up watching these guys." She bumped shoulders with Cole. "Football, baseball, basketball, track, one of them was always playing something. Softball was my thing. So, much to Gram's disappointment, I'm for the sports center."

"Your grandmother remembers the Anderson family. She'd like to see them honored for their generosity."

"Right, and the sports complex makes the most of those funds, which is the best way to honor Anderson." Cole said, and then polished off his last bite of pie.

"And around and round we go. We have a sports complex. If we need the fancy misting system and such, why haven't we done something about it before now?"

"No money for it. The endowment makes it possible. Plus a bigger and better complex will draw tournaments, which will bring in revenue, not only to the town coffers, but to the local merchants, too. Within a few years the town will be able to do a lot more to improve the community. Including a scaled-down museum and garden if the citizens want it."

He made it sound so simple, so sane.

"The museum and garden will be a source of revenue, as well, with the rooms and garden space rented out for social occasions and community events."

Cole shook his head. "Social occasions around here are mostly backyard barbecues. The reality is that the upkeep of the garden would probably be a strain on the economy and, in drought years like this, a drain on our water resources, as well."

"That's unfair." Outraged, Dani hit the table, causing the gentleman behind Mattie to turn and check out their booth. Paying no attention to him, Dani argued her point. "The fields at the sports complex would require the same care and water."

"No. The fields are dirt and grass with a few hardy bushes and trees that the local teams can help maintain to offset expenses. A landscaped botanical garden would require one, maybe two, full-time professional gardeners and a specialized irrigation system."

The authority in his tone, the confidence in his posture reminded her this was what Cole did. As a landscaper and nursery owner, he obviously knew what he was talking about, leaving her little room to argue.

The gentleman eavesdropping quickly picked up on her hesitation.

"That's right, Lady Candidate, that garden is a money hole. Paradise Pines can't afford to pour money into a useless venture, no matter how pretty it is."

From there, one diner then another chimed in with an opinion until shouts were being traded across the room. Dani did her best to represent the values of education, tradition and history, but she was nearly drowned out by coaches, proud dads and the odd soccer mom.

The derisive attitude sparked several women to speak up in defense of Dani. She sent Cole a sidelong look. She noticed he did nothing to add to the melee, but he did nothing to stop it either. He caught her gaze and she cocked her head toward the vocal locals.

"See," she said.

"What?" he responded, all innocent.

"You're too smart to be able to play dumb. Your followers aren't so sharp. The women are rallying in response to the men's attitude. What a Woman Wants will be packed tomorrow." She gathered her purse and slid to the edge of the booth. "Every time this happens, I gain supporters. I don't really want to win this race, but at this rate, I just might. You want to win? Then it's the men who need to be handled, not the women." She stood. "I have to get home to Faith."

"I'll walk you to your car." He unfolded his six-foot-plus frame from the booth.

Dani stepped away from the heat and male scent of him. "That's not necessary."

"My grandmother would say it was and I'm already in her doghouse. I'm not going to disrespect the manners she taught me." He tossed a twenty on the table and waved to Mattie.

Outside, fall nipped in the air, cool, crisp

and pine scented, a far cry from the dry chill of Phoenix. Dani savored the knowledge she'd escaped the desert metropolis.

The border drug trafficking had turned her hometown into a violent, crime-ridden city. Maybe not to the level of New York or L.A., but bad enough she'd felt the need to move Faith away from the city that had stolen her father's life.

Dani stopped next to her car and turned to Cole, realizing they'd strolled the half block in companionable silence.

How was that possible when the man rubbed all her nerves wrong?

"This is me." She gestured to her car. "Thanks for the escort." She, too, had been taught manners.

"Let me." He took her keys from her and moved to the driver's door.

She started to protest but that would only prolong the process. Really, she just wanted to go home.

She waited for him to step away from the open door, but he didn't. Instead he dangled her keys and waved for her to take her seat.

For his own perverse amusement he'd been playing with her all night. Well, enough.

She stormed forward, snatched her keys from him and invaded his space.

"Just so we're clear, this was not a date. We had coffee. We're invested together as godparents for Jake, otherwise we are opponents. It's best if we restrict our interaction to the christening classes."

"Dani." He took her hand, lifted her arm and twirled her around in a move smooth as a turn in a waltz, delivering her into her seat with a warm hand in the small of her back. "I thoroughly enjoyed the evening, but we're opponents more than you think."

Stunned to find herself behind the wheel, she gazed up at him. "What do you mean?"

"It's simple, my lovely." Still holding her hand, he lowered his dark head to kiss the back of her fingers before whispering, "I don't want to win either."

Then with a wink and a wave, he sauntered away.

CHAPTER FOUR

As Dani predicted, by ten-thirty the next morning What A Woman Wants was crowded with women shopping, primping and lamenting the backward thinking of the Paradise Pines male population.

The conversation had been building steam for a while when the blonde in Dani's chair looked through the mirror at Dani and said, "I was just trying to say a museum wasn't such a bad idea, that we're always saying how the kids today are all into instant gratification. And if we stopped and talked about the past sometimes, it might slow them down a little and give them an appreciation of how we got to where we are today. And my husband says to me, don't be stupid and I better not be voting for no museum."

Dani winced.

"Yeah." The woman nodded, causing her hair to slip from between Dani's fingers. "I showed him stupid this morning when I forgot to make his lunch."

"I know." A woman at one of the nail stations spoke up. "It's not like I expect my husband to vote for the museum, but I do expect to be allowed my own opinion."

The stylist next to Dani turned off the blow dryer she wielded to point it and declare. "That's right. This is the twenty-first century, not the turn of the century. We earned the right to vote a long time ago."

"I think Blondie's got the right idea," Mrs. Day piped up. She'd pushed the bonnet dryer up so she could hear. "If we want to be heard, we need to hit the men where it hurts."

"Yeah," another voice chirped. "I bet he notices when his lunch is missing."

Dani had a bad feeling about where this was going.

"Well, to be fair," she interjected, "nobody is stopping any of us from voting."

"No, but they're trying to tell us how to vote. That's just as bad."

"Worse, they're trying to tell us how to think. If we let them get away with this, we'll wipe out a hundred years' worth of struggle for women's rights."

"Yeah. Paradise Pines will be the most backward town in the whole U.S.A."

"We have to hit them where it hurts," Mrs. Day suggested with a tad more vehemence than necessary. "No cooking and no cleaning. We'll remind them what life was like in the dark ages of their bachelor days."

"Let's do it. No cooking. No cleaning." The women began to chant.

Dani held up the curling iron in her hand, demanding silence. "If we're going to do this, everyone has to participate or the impact will be lost. No wimping out."

Emphatic nods followed her decree and they went on to plan their attack.

Now this was the fight Dani believed in. The museum and garden was a lovely thought but, for all practical purposes, doomed before they got started. Which didn't mean it didn't deserve a spot on the ballot. It was the insulting dismissal of their entire agenda that fueled the fight. The right to be heard, to be respected—yeah, this battle Dani would fight every time.

Their methods may be archaic but then so

was the men's attitude. They said the way to a man's heart was through his stomach. With any luck it was also the way to reach their hard heads.

In church on Sunday morning, Dani discovered a couple of the Sullivan men had lovely baritones. Cole wasn't one of them. Did that stop him from singing? Of course not. And his flawed enthusiasm made his efforts more genuine. More charming.

She ought to know, as she stood almost shoulder to shoulder with him, separated only by the squat presence of her matchmaking daughter. The little punk had grabbed his hand and then her mother's, making sure they all sat together.

Which wouldn't be a problem, except the man kept finding ways to get to her without even trying.

She and Faith had been invited to church followed by Sunday dinner at the Sullivans'. As a future godparent to one of the Sullivan brood, Dani felt it prudent to accept. Expecting it to be the women and children attending, the presence of Cole and two of his brothers surprised her. In her experience men weren't big on attending services, but then faith had never really been a big part of her life.

Obviously it was for the Sullivans, from the toddlers who were well behaved and respectful to the adults who followed the readings in the missal but knew the prayers and songs by heart. Sunday services and family togetherness meant something to them.

It made Dani feel a part of something special. And this service, more than the christening classes, made her realize the role she'd taken on as godparent really was an honor and a responsibility.

For the first time in a long time, she bowed her head and prayed. She gave thanks for her beautiful, meddling, loving daughter and then asked for guidance, strength and the wisdom to make good decisions.

A soft snore on the other side of Dani had her turning toward Samantha. Her head listed slightly to the side and her even breathing betrayed her snoozing.

Dani nudged her friend with a gentle elbow.

Samantha started, blinked and grimaced at Dani. "Thanks," she whispered.

Dani nodded. She'd noticed the shadows

under her friend's eyes earlier and determined to find out what was causing Samantha's fatigue when they got a chance to talk.

When the congregation turned to wish each other peace, simple handshakes and well wishes were exchanged, but like everything else the Sullivans amped it up, adding hugs and kisses to the mix. For Dani, unused to demonstrative shows of affection, it was a bit awkward but not unpleasant.

Until she turned and met Cole's amused blue gaze. Immediately she saw he'd clued into her reticence. Showing him she could be a good sport, she lifted her head for his kiss on the cheek. At the last moment he turned his head and lightly brushed his mouth over hers.

"Peace be with you," he said softly, as if he hadn't just sent her entire system into emotional turmoil.

The punk opportunist had sneaked a smooch in the middle of church. He ought to be ashamed. She narrowed her eyes at him before bending to give her daughter a kiss. Yeah, much more her speed.

An hour later she sat with Samantha at a

backyard patio table watching the Sullivan men man the barbecue.

She pointed to them. "How did Gram get the guys to cook without giving away the whole make-them-listen plan?"

Samantha smothered a yawn then grinned. "She simply told them it was time to give the women a break and they'd be cooking and doing the cleanup today. They didn't question her at all, just started talking about what they'd grill." She swept a glance over the playing kids before settling her attention back on Dani, a determined glint in her eyes. "So I saw Cole plant one on you in church. What's with the two of you?"

"Nothing." Dani immediately denied any connection between her and Cole. "So don't get your hopes up. He likes to mess with my mind is all. He doesn't mean anything with his flirting."

"He kissed you in church, in front of his family," Samantha emphasized. "Cole doesn't mix family and flirting."

"Come on." Dani sent her friend an arch glance. "We both know he's a master opportunist. He saw an opening and he took it."

"Well, yeah, but it doesn't mean he wasn't serious. He kissed you in full view of Gram. I think he was declaring his intentions."

Now there was a scary thought. His persistent playfulness and pretend come-ons already had her wanting things she couldn't have, reminding her of how good it had been to be held, to have someone to share her concerns with.

Dani shook her head. "He's already told me I'm not his type, and he couldn't be more right. He's all play and I'm all business."

"It's a known fact, opposites attract."

Dani shook a finger at Sami. "I'm not marrying one of the Sullivans just to make you happy. We're as good as sisters already."

"I know. I just missed you so much after I moved here, and now that we're back together I don't want to lose you again."

"You didn't lose me before. At first you were busy fighting for Gabe and then I was grieving for Kevin. You came over to Phoenix as soon as you heard he'd been killed, helped me through the hardest week of my life." Her voice grew husky as memories of that horrible time, of her overwhelming loss, rushed at her. "I don't know what Faith and I would have done without you."

Samantha covered Dani's hand with her own and squeezed. Dani pressed her lips tight together, fighting for control. She drew in a deep breath, released it slowly, pushing the tears back.

"You were there every time I needed you. That's not going to change whether I'm in Paradise Pines or not, or if I'm married to one of the Sullivans or not. And I hope you know I'll always be there for you."

"I know," Samantha allowed. "Of course I know, but I love you and I love them. They really are good guys, and I want to see you happy."

"I am happy."

Samantha tilted her head and looked at Dani over her sunglasses. The direct gaze made Dani squirm in her seat.

"All right. But I couldn't handle happy right now. It's all I can do to handle Faith and the shop. And now I have to fit a political campaign in, too. Tell me again why you didn't talk me out of that craziness."

"Maybe because you agreed to do it before I heard anything about it."

"Maybe." Dani glanced over to where Cole strolled through the yard with Gram. She carried a ruffle-edged umbrella. He wore garden gloves and occasionally bent to prune a plant or pull a weed.

As Dani watched he threw back his head, laughing at something his grandmother said. For all their public dispute, the love between them showed in his gentleness, in her tolerance, and in their shared laughter. Whatever the outcome of the upcoming election, that love wouldn't change.

Dani barely comprehended that kind of family support and commitment. If it weren't for Faith, Dani wouldn't even recognize what she was seeing.

She thought of Cole's parting shot the other night and wondered if he truly didn't want to win the election, or if he was messing with her yet again.

Refusing to let him ruin her day, she turned her back to him, hoping out of sight would be out of mind, and asked Samantha what had her snoozing in church. For the next thirty minutes she listened to Samantha vent about Jake's cold, Seth's potty training, Gabe's preschool antics, and the ongoing bickering of the Harvest dance committee. The last made Dani glad she'd refused her friend's request to co-chair the event.

That was one time she'd made the right decision. Then again, if she'd been working on the dance committee, she'd probably have said no to running for office.

Maybe there were no right decisions.

Right, and she could just hear Cole saying that meant there were no wrong decisions, there was just life.

No, she couldn't believe that. The right decisions allowed her some control, and she'd take any advantage she could get.

"You ought to be ashamed," Gram admonished Cole as they strolled through the yard looking over her garden. "Making a move on a girl in church. It's something a fifteen-year-old would do."

Cole laughed. "I was never so smooth at fifteen."

"You're missing my point."

"Come on. You taught us church was a place to celebrate life. I don't think the good Lord is up there shaking a finger at me for kissing a girl."

"He might be if you're going to hurt that girl. She's known a lot of pain in her short life. She doesn't need any more."

He rose from where he'd pruned weeds away from her blooming dahlias, his gaze going to the patio table where Dani sat talking with Samantha. Her hair flowed over her shoulder in a lush auburn fall, a beautiful frame for her creamy complexion.

"I'm not looking to hurt her," he said.

"Just because you don't intend to doesn't mean you won't. Do you have feelings for her?" Gram held open a trash bag for the weeds.

He hesitated, then tossed the weeds and dusted his gloved hands together. "I like spending time with her."

"Hmm." Gram hummed in her maternal way. "Why? Is she someone you could leave your plants with?"

For a moment he didn't follow her and then it clicked. Annoyed after he ended a brief fling with a woman Gram particularly liked, she'd asked him what it would take for him to finally settle down. He'd replied he'd settle down when he found a woman he could trust his plants with.

She hadn't been amused.

He'd been serious. How a person handled a plant said a lot about them.

So, of course, the sad rubber plant in Dani's shop immediately came to mind. He shook his head. Crouching to examine the bed of dormant roses, he considered Gram's question.

"She's pretty, bright and a good mother. What's not to like."

Gram nodded, her gaze knowing. "Yes, she's a good mother, which is usually enough to send you in the opposite direction."

"I like kids." His back went up.

"Yes, you're lovely with children." She brushed the hair back over his ear, a gesture of love. "But not usually in connection with the women you date."

He pushed to his feet. "It was just a little kiss, Gram. It didn't mean anything."

Before Dani knew it, the men were calling out that the food was ready. Chaos reigned as everyone attacked the great barbecue fare. The guys had roasted corn and potatoes along with the chicken on the grill and one of them dumped a bag of salad into a bowl. Simple but good.

Faith loved corn on the cob and it showed all down the front of her. Dani just shook her head and grinned at her baby. By the time she and the other women got the kids cleaned up, the men had the kitchen spic-and-span.

Dani sat relaxing with Samantha and her two sisters-in-law at the large dining room table in the family room when the men came in to join them. Dani took that as a sign to be leaving soon. Across the table, Cole was way too close.

Not wanting to be rude by eating and running, she promised herself she'd leave in twenty minutes.

Ford, the youngest Sullivan, teased Samantha about falling asleep in church, and Dani soon found the Sullivans, both men and women, lived up to Samantha's hype of them. Laughter flowed as easy as the conversation and much to Dani's personal joy none of it focused around the sports complex or museum/garden proposals.

When she glanced at her watch again, the better part of an hour had slipped past.

"I should go," she told the table at large. "It's way past Faith's nap time."

"No," Samantha protested. "It's early yet.

We're going to play a game and we need you for the numbers. Besides, Gram probably already has the kids settled down."

Now she mentioned it, there was an absence of shrill squeals, toys pounding, and shared giggles. "Oh, but—"

Gram stuck her head in from the living room. "I put Faith down with the boys for their naps. Just checked on them a few minutes ago and they're like candles, all light and bright one moment and out the next."

"Oh, well." Dani pondered the moment. Her plan to leave revolved more around getting away from Cole than anything else. She stole a glance his way. More than once she'd felt him watching her, the awareness of him a low-level buzz to her system.

But mostly he'd been behaving himself and she did enjoy spending time with these sharp and funny adults. It felt like forever since she had spent more than a few minutes in mixed company. Even at events like today, she usually visited with the women and then took her leave.

"Stay," Samantha entreated. "Play with us."

"Okay, I guess it'll be fun. I haven't played a game since you left Phoenix."

"Oh, yeah," Cole's older brother Brock said. "Samantha's the one that brought a whole new meaning to the words *game day* for the Sullivans. Used to be these afternoons were lazy days to watch whatever sports were playing. Now once a month we sit down and play a game."

"Yeah, I miss the good old days." Cole sighed.

"Shut it, you slug." Ford kicked out at Cole's chair, already tipped back on two legs. "Nobody's holding your feet to the flame to be here."

Cole had to grab the table to keep from going over backward. "Rachel, are you going to let him get away with that?"

"Of course not." Rachel swept platinum-blond bangs out of her eyes, leaned over the corner of the table to reach her husband and, pulling him close, kissed him with heated intent. After a minute, she let him go and licked her lips. "Sweetie, you don't have to play if you don't want to."

"Oh, I want to play," Ford responded, a flush in his cheeks and a huskiness to his voice.

"I thought so. Now leave Cole alone."

Dani must have looked slightly bug-eyed,

because Jesse explained, "It's not as bad as they're making it sound. Once a month the guys give up whatever sporting event is on for the day and we play a game. Trivial Pursuit, poker, whatever. But the guys get to pick the week, and they get to have one game on TV—on mute." She nodded to the big-screen set in the corner of the family room. Dani had seen all of the men sneak a peak at the set during their conversation.

"And—" Samantha picked up the explanation with a wry glance at each of the men "—if one of them gets a text from one of their contacts that there's a particularly good game going, we all quit and watch."

"We have a lot of fun," Rachel said. "And we all get to keep in touch with each other. Even getting together for Sunday dinners, it's easy to miss connecting with everyone every week."

"Mattie usually takes off Sundays so she can participate." Alex set a Trivial Pursuit box in the middle of the table. "But the diner has been packed this week."

"Yeah, I was talking to her yesterday." Ford opened the box and began sorting out the pieces. "She said it was like half the town went on strike and refused to cook."

Across the table, Cole went still then slowly lifted his gaze. His blue eyes narrowed on Dani. "Interesting phenomenon."

For a moment it was as if they were the only two in the room. Dani smiled, showing all her teeth. "Why yes. How odd."

"It almost sounds like something someone planned."

She lifted her brows. "Now why would anyone have cause to do that?"

"No politics at the game table." Samantha laid down the law.

Dani had no problem with that, especially as Jesse announced from the other end of the table that because there were so many of them, they played in pairs. Dani had the bad feeling that as odd man and woman out she and Cole would be coupled together.

She sighed in relief to learn they drew names to make up the pairs. It was the women's turn to draw names and she was thrilled when she got Alex. Of all the men, she knew him best.

Turned out they were good partners and, with much laughter, some debate and a few lucky rolls of the dice, they took an early lead.

The group took a break about halfway through the game because the guys wanted dessert. Ford and Brock volunteered to dish up, keeping with the women's-day-off theme, but Rachel and Jesse joined them in the kitchen to supervise.

Seeing Samantha yawn, Dani nudged her partner. "Alex, I think you need to take your wife away for a weekend of rest and relaxation."

Samantha perked up. Alex looked at his wife with a gleam in his eyes and said, "There's an idea."

Cole nudged Samantha a couple of times and wiggled his eyebrows. "Sami, you should take Alex away for a weekend of hot passion."

Samantha flushed pink and she looked at Alex with longing. "That sounds wonderful."

"I do have the conference in New Orleans in mid-November," Alex said. "You could fly over and join me for the weekend."

Excitement lit Samantha up, but the glow quickly faded as resignation claimed her momentary radiance. "I can't. The kids."

"Oh, please," Dani huffed. "That better not be your excuse. I can watch the kids."

Samantha shook her head. "I can't ask you to do that. With the three boys and Faith, it would be too much."

"You didn't ask, I offered. I'm sure I can handle it for a few days."

"No, they come with too much stuff, and the baby has a cold—"

"So I'll go to your house." Samantha did so much for Dani that she really wanted to help her friend out. "And I'm sure Jake will be feeling better by mid-November. Come on, Faith practically lives at your place. Let me do this for you."

Still Samantha hesitated. "You don't know how much trouble three boys can be twenty-four/seven."

"I'll help her," Cole chimed in. "Between the two of us we should be fine."

"Oh, but—" Dani protested, horrified by the idea. But Samantha talked right over her.

"That would be great." Samantha jumped up and threw her arms around Cole, giving him a big kiss on the cheek.

"Hey, I'm the one supposed to get the passion." Alex pulled his wife away from his brother and swung her into a steamy clinch.

Glancing away from the embracing

couple, Dani caught a look of acute envy on Cole's face as he watched his brother and Samantha. For a moment he appeared the picture of loneliness. She turned away, giving him privacy, understanding only too well how being alone ate at the soul.

Laughing softly, the couple broke apart, flushed and pleased with themselves. A few minutes later the others returned to the table with plates of chocolate cake, and the game resumed.

That night doing laundry, Dani admitted she had enjoyed taking the win from Cole and Jesse. She'd had a good time today. And so had Faith. Several times Dani saw her dancing around Cole, climbing into his lap, giggling as she whispered in his ear. Her affection for him was totally on her sleeve, as was his for her.

But Dani also saw how he gave Faith a couple of minutes of his attention, and then sent her back to play with the other kids, more than once with a slightly wistful expression.

Dani sighed. He really was a decent guy.

CHAPTER FIVE

SHORTLY AFTER SHE PUT Faith down to sleep, a knock sounded at Dani's door. By the height and profile visible through the half medallion of smoky glass in her door, her visitor must be a man. One tall, lean, frustrating male by her guess, a hunch confirmed when she spied Cole through the peephole.

The man was a relentless pest, which didn't stop her from licking her lips and fluffing her hair before opening the door a scant three inches.

"Cole," she acknowledged, trying for cold and forbidding but achieving breathy. "What do you want? Here to steal another kiss?"

Was she crazy? Why had she brought that up? Ignoring the felonious smooch would be far smarter.

"Sure, if you're offering." The door proved

no barrier when he leaned down and snagged her mouth with his.

Dani moaned under the soft ravishment of his lips. No simple peck like in church, this kiss pulled a response from her. He didn't press but finessed, sipping, teasing, drawing her latent passion to the surface.

Oh, yeah, this was crazy good.

They touched only where her mouth clung to his, the door still mostly between them. And she wanted more, wanted his arms around her, his body next to hers.

Sweet sugar cookies, she longed to get her hands on him.

So, of course, she pushed him away. Okay, he had already started lifting his head, but she preferred to stick with her version and retain a little self-respect.

Her breathing fogged the cool night air between them as she tried to calm her wildly beating heart.

He made no attempt to enter the house, simply leaned against the doorjamb, far too close and far too happy with himself.

She scowled. "So why are you here again?"

He lifted a dark eyebrow, and the porch

light caught the leap of passion in his eyes as he inched closer.

"Do you want me to show you again?"

She planted a hand in the center of his chest, holding him at a distance even as she thrilled to feel his heart thundering under her fingers.

"Speak or leave."

"So cold. You're not going to invite me in?"

"I'm glad we're both clear on that."

He blinked, refocused, and then flashed his pearly whites at her. "You could come out here with me."

"I guess you're leaving, then. Good night."

"Wait." His warm grip settled over hers on the door, not pushing, just touching. "I came to confirm I was right. The museum group is playing some kind of game by not cooking. Tell me I'm wrong."

"You're the enemy. I'm not telling you anything, except the supporters of the museum and garden proposal genuinely care about the outcome of this vote. It's not a game to them, and it would be a mistake not to take them seriously."

Solemn, he nodded. But of course he

didn't mean it. "I knew it. Whose wild idea was this? Seems a little desperate to me."

"Underdogs need to be inventive." Why was she allowing this conversation to continue? Probably because her senses were still spinning from his kiss. The thought of spending a whole weekend in his combustible company shook her to the core. She should call him on his offer, let him know she didn't want or need his help, but she didn't have the energy. Didn't have the guts.

"If that's all, I'm getting cold."

"No, you aren't." He feathered the back of a finger along her cheekbone, caught a loose tendril and tucked it behind her ear. "You're feeling the heat. Just like me."

"Cole—"

"You don't have to be afraid of me." His voice was soft; his eyes told her she could trust him. But even his cousin said he was full of sweet talk and hot air.

"Haven't you guessed, everything scares me these days?" Pulling her hand free of his, she slowly closed and locked the door.

"I don't know why those women are against the sports complex, 'cause they're not opposed to playing games," Doc Wilcox groused. He and Palmer and the two other members of Cole's campaign committee were packed into the mayor's office.

Cole controlled the urge to snap that the endowment issue wasn't a game and that the opposing camp was entitled to their own opinions and the corresponding strategies to bring about the vote they were looking for. It didn't matter that he'd said nearly the same thing to Dani on Sunday. That conversation had just been between the two of them. And truthfully the topic was more an excuse than a reason for stopping at her place.

He'd told her she wasn't his type, which couldn't be more true. He was loose and easy and she was tightly wound and overcommitted. But Lord, he did enjoy pushing her buttons.

Sunday night he'd wanted to push a few buttons free on her pale blue blouse, reveal her creamy loveliness, touch her baby-soft skin.

She tried so hard to fight him, and then she'd stop and call his bluff. He loved it when she stood up to him.

Whoa, wait. He shifted restlessly in his chair. Love had nothing to do with his feelings for Dani. She was fun, that was all.

So he enjoyed having her at Gram's for Sunday dinner. He could admire a pretty woman sitting in the shade of an umbrella on a hot afternoon simply for the beauty of the moment. It didn't mean he was ready to pick out china patterns with her.

And so what if he'd blown the winning question of the trivia game because he was distracted by the way her teeth bit into her plump bottom lip while she anxiously awaited the answer. There was no harm in looking.

"I didn't even notice my wife had stopped cleaning." Palmer adjusted his tie. "I was just glad not to have the vacuum running during the game."

"What about the no cooking?" Julie Barnes, his office manager, asked. "You didn't notice that?"

"Sure." Palmer shrugged. "But I didn't marry her for her cooking, if you know what I mean."

Cole blocked out the debate. Man, he should never have kissed Dani. Not even a little peck on the lips. Because now he knew how sweet she tasted, and he wanted more.

He'd been insane to kiss her in church. That was too close to the altar for comfort.

Not to mention Gram had seen the whole thing, leaving him wide open for a lecture about the inappropriateness of his actions during their weekly stroll around the garden. Church was not the place to make a move on a woman. And what were his intentions anyway?

Good question. Or not. He liked Dani, enjoyed her company. Neither required a commitment on his part. Or hers. A good thing, because from the way she had closed the door on him last Sunday, clearly she wasn't going to give him a chance.

He liked being his own boss, thrived on being a free agent, on not answering to anyone. Sure he loved his family and he considered them a close bunch, but he made his own decisions and his relationships were his own business.

Cole was a puzzle enthusiast; he thrived on the challenge of finding pieces to form the big picture, which was why he loved landscaping. And was probably what made him so good at playing the stock market, and had helped him warn the family when the economy crashed. More his obsession of puzzles fed his other great passion.

He loved women, always had, always would. From little beauties like Faith to his grandmother's oldest friend, Miss Betty, he found women enchanting and mysterious, an ever-present puzzle wrapped in lovely packaging. They were such a contradiction of traits, soft yet fierce, strong and resilient, prone to laughter and tears, often at the same time. In any given moment you never knew what you were going to get from them.

Women were the ultimate puzzle.

Yeah, he loved them. In the plural. He enjoyed their company, some more intimately than others, their intense emotions, their hare-brained reasoning, and all varieties in between. But he didn't get serious with any of them.

And he didn't bring women home to Gram.

He made no apologies because he liked to keep it casual. So what if he occasionally longed for what his brothers had found with their wives. Or if he experienced a twinge of loneliness every now and again. He preferred to keep it simple until the right woman came along.

Which was no reason for the memory of Dani in her sleeveless blue blouse and white miniskirt sitting at his grandmother's table to pop into his mind.

"So Cole," Wilcox said, pulling Cole's attention back to the conversation. "What are we going to do to combat this no-cooking, no-cleaning campaign of theirs?"

"Nothing." Annoyed with the topic, Cole tapped the end of his pen against his blotter.

"We have to do something," Palmer protested.

"They just want to be heard, to have their opinions validated," Cole stated.

"Right," Julie agreed. "It's a personal issue for many of them. If we make it a public issue, it gives weight to their argument." She waved a hand, indicating Palmer. "And if the men aren't even noticing, then their plan is failing anyway."

"They want a museum and botanical garden," Wilcox argued. "If we ignore their efforts, they may gain momentum, especially if their strategy begins to work."

"We could invite them to participate in a public debate. Give them the sense of being heard," Julie mused. "Ours is the stronger position. Letting them speak would show them up as the weaker choice."

"Who's going to pay for this debate?" Cole's accounting manager asked. "Public meetings are expensive."

"We can add it to an already scheduled city event. That'll bring the expenses down and guarantee an audience."

"I still say you're making too big an issue of this. We need to stay focused on our own agenda." The last thing Cole wanted was a public showdown with Dani.

"A debate is inevitable." Doc Wilcox threw in his approval of the public meeting. "It may as well be now when it's to our advantage. But let's keep it small, control the venue."

"We need to get our plans out there." Cole tried a new argument. "Let the people of Paradise Pines see the beautiful facility we have drafted. That's what's going to win us this election."

"You're right, and the debate will be the perfect place to hand out flyers. Great, we're decided." Palmer rubbed his hands together. "Julie, you start looking for an event we can piggyback on. I'll make up the flyers. Cole, you issue an official invitation to the Wilder woman. She ought to be thrilled to participate."

With a sigh of resignation, Cole settled back in his chair. Thrilled? He didn't think so.

"Can we get a really big pumpkin, Mommy? One this big?" Faith held her little arms above her head.

Dani tickled her daughter's ribs as she pulled a pink sweater into place over the upraised arms. She laughed along with Faith, loving the sound of her giggles.

"I don't know. That's an awfully big pumpkin. Mommy's got to be able to carry it to the car."

"You can do it, Mommy. You're strong."

If only that were true. But it thrilled her that Faith thought so. "We'll see."

"Weelll…"

Dani waited, knowing the drawn-out word meant her precocious daughter's active mind was at work.

"If you can't carry the big pumpkin, maybe you can get the man with the nice butt to help you."

"Faith Marie," Dani exclaimed, shocked. "You do not say *butt*."

"I didn't say it Mommy, you did. The last

time we went to the nursery. You said the man in the hat had a really nice—"

"Stop," Dani demanded. "You don't get to say it again." Her little girl loved to learn new words and repeat the forbidden; she'd wrap this conversation back on itself several times if Dani let her, sneaking the bad word in a couple of more times with creative flair.

Dani knew exactly when she had made the fatal slip. In late summer they'd been at Sullivan's Garden and Landscaping to pick up some potting soil and a few fall blooms. The place was huge, not only rows of plants, but fields, including a hillside of budding pumpkins and a pine forest of Christmas trees. Sullivan's catered to both the home gardener and professionals.

It had been hot that day and in the distance a man in a wide-brimmed hat had worked the pumpkin patch. He wore a sleeveless white tank, low-riding jeans and gardening gloves. Tanned and fit, his arms flexed with muscles as he labored. Her gaze had been drawn to him again and again. She especially enjoyed the back view when he bent or squatted to work the field.

She didn't remember admiring his backside out loud, but evidently she had. She did remember lingering over her choice of plants longer than necessary hoping to catch a glimpse of his face, but he'd stayed on the hillside.

Lord save her, she now knew she'd been ogling Cole Sullivan, which twisted her up in so many knots. How much easier her life had been when he was simply a fantasy in a pumpkin patch.

His kiss haunted her. In those few minutes she'd felt alive again, as if life had meaning and purpose, as if she were young with a promising future. She'd longed to leap through the door and grab a hold of him with both arms.

At the same time everything in her wanted to cling to the past, to the memory of the husband she'd loved and lost too soon. She couldn't let him go, who else would keep him alive for Faith?

With that thought she turned her attention back to her baby and tried to regain control of the situation.

"Mommy shouldn't have said that word either. Especially not when big ears could hear." She tugged on tiny earlobes.

Faith giggled and covered her ears. "I don't have big ears." She grinned at Dani. "You didn't think I was hearing, but I was."

"Listening," Dani automatically corrected her. "You were listening."

"What does *lissening* mean?"

"Listening—" Dani emphasized the pronunciation— "means when you hear something, you're paying attention."

"Yep, I was lissening," she confirmed, plopping on her rear end to put on her shoes, pink Mary Janes with princess tiaras on the heels.

"And you're listening now, too, when Mommy is telling you not to say that word again, right?"

"Yes, Mommy. Is this the right foot?" And that was that, life moved on. At least for Faith. And, of course, it wasn't the right foot, Faith being a little dyslexic when it came to her feet.

Soon they were loaded into the car, tooling along to Sullivan's Garden and Landscaping.

Thoughts of escaping to a commercial pumpkin lot in El Cajon or San Diego tempted Dani, but it smacked of cowardice. Because she wouldn't be taking Faith to have fun in the big jumping balloon or to play the carnival games. No, she'd be fleeing the prospect of running into Cole.

She hadn't seen him to talk to since he'd kissed her on her doorstep a week ago. He'd stopped by her shop to see her, but she'd been out to the bank. He hadn't left a message, and he hadn't come back.

She'd been totally and inappropriately disappointed she'd missed him. Which was exactly why she was avoiding him.

But not today. She wanted Faith to have the organic experience of picking a pumpkin from a real pumpkin patch. The two of them spent a lot of time in their tiny yard, building a garden that was both beautiful to look at and fun to play in. Dani did most the work and Faith most of the playing, and that suited Dani just fine. She found peace in the garden and she loved to see the plants and flowers bloom and grow, knowing she created such beauty. Plus the sun and exercise were good for her and Faith.

"Are we there yet?" a small voice demanded from the backseat.

"Yep, but I almost don't recognize the place."

As she pulled in to the parking lot, she saw

the commercial lots had nothing on Cole. Complete with a jumping balloon in the shape of a yellow barn, Sullivan's had been converted into an old-fashioned farm.

Faith struggled to see out the window. "Wow, Mommy, there's a jumper. And cows and ponies." She hopped in her car seat. "Can I go in the jumper? Can I ride a pony?"

"Those aren't cows, they're goats." Dani parked and helped Faith from her seat. "Do you want your stroller?"

"No, I want to walk. I want to see everything."

"Okay, let's go." Dani took her hand. "It looks like there's a lot to see. Let's wander around first, to see what's here."

With Faith skipping at her side, Dani led them inside. It was like walking into a new world. Sawdust and straw littered the walkways. Scarecrows greeted them and pointed the way toward the back of the lot where plants had been replaced by a mini petting zoo and the big yellow bouncing barn. Refreshment booths and autumn and Halloween displays lined the path. Farther along, a hayride took people out to the pumpkin patch.

Her gaze kept going up and, above the pumpkins, the hill rose another hundred feet to where a large house tucked into the surrounding pines sat at the top. With sprawling decks and a whole wall of windows reflecting the late-morning sun, Dani thought it probably had one of the best views in the whole valley.

Tugging on her hand, Faith led Dani toward the petting zoo. "Can I pet the goats? Please."

"Oh, really?" Dani hid a grimace. She and goats, not the best of friends and she had the scar to prove it. For Faith, she'd bite the bullet, but maybe the girl could be distracted. "I thought you wanted to ride a pony."

"I want to do both."

Of course she did.

"Well, now, how are two of my favorite ladies?" Cole appeared beside them. He traced a finger down Faith's cheek. "Don't you look pretty in pink?"

"Cole!" She threw her arms around his knees. "I missed you."

With a chiding look at Dani, he bent to pick Faith up and give her a kiss on the cheek. "I've missed you, too. Are you going to go in and pet the animals? There are bunnies inside."

"Baby bunnies?" Faith asked in awe.

He shared a grin with Dani, causing her heart to twist at how wonderful he was with her daughter. His gentleness and patience put Faith at ease. More, he encouraged her to explore her world and expand her mind.

"Yep, baby bunnies. Would you like to pet them?"

"Yes, please."

Her polite response made Dani proud. Her excited giggle made Dani sweat. She rubbed the scar on her left index finger and eyed the enclosure anxiously. She was going to have to face the goats.

"Why don't I take her to see the goats and bunnies while you get us some popcorn and lemonade?" Cole suggested.

Surprised by the offer, she met his gaze. Understanding blended with an overt awareness and something else she didn't recognize but warmed her insides. He'd noted her distress and offered an out.

"Hi," he said.

"Hi," she responded softly, feeling the world narrow to just them. Lord help her, she missed him as much as Faith did.

"Purple looks good on you, and I like the

skirt." Holding her gaze, he reached out, fingering a loose strand of hair near her cheek. She felt the pull and wished for his touch. "You make a sexy gypsy."

"Then I'm right at home." She made a show of looking around. "This is quite a party you have going on."

His gaze never left her. "Yeah, it's fun. Good business, too, though it's only evenings and weekends. There are booths where the kids can do crafts or paint a pumpkin, and there's face painting. Faith will like that."

"Yeah, she will. I hope I brought enough money for all this."

"You'll be fine. The booths, including the face painting, are free. The food vendors charge, but they're all locals and they keep it reasonable. We just want everyone to have a good time."

She lifted an eyebrow at him. "A happy customer is more free with his money?"

"So I've found. I love the holidays. It's my busy time of year. Not only do we have the festivities here, but my landscape clients want their buildings and grounds decorated for the holidays." Pride rang in every word he spoke and in the way he surveyed his land

and business. "After Halloween we have a harvest festival with craft booths, and from Thanksgiving through the end of the year we switch to a winter theme. The pumpkin patch is turned into a snow hill and Marty brings the petting zoo back with reindeer."

"Wow, I'm impressed."

His animation, the pride in his expression, the way he made nature an adventure for his customers all told her he loved what he did.

She nodded toward the far pumpkin patch. "I've seen you working the grounds out here."

His eyes lit up and his fingers flexed. "Every chance I get. I saw your rubber plant was doing better."

"Yes, much better. Thanks for the advice. I'm sorry I was out when you came by." Jeez, lame maybe? But she couldn't outright say she missed him. They were competitors after all. "Was there something you needed?"

He shook his head. "I'm not dealing with that here. Not today."

Something to do with the election, then. Of course it would be. So why the instant letdown? Didn't matter. She shook it off, agreeing with him. Not here, not today.

She nodded. "Okay."

"Mommy, the bunnies!" An impatient Faith demanded their attention.

"Right, baby. I'm sorry." Time to man up.

"Dani, really, I can handle this." Cole offered again.

She lifted her chin. So stupid to be afraid of a simple farm animal. "I don't mind the bunnies," she said.

Trying hard not to appear a wuss in front of him, she almost missed the flash of resigned disappointment on Cole's face. She'd given him such a hard time about spending time with Faith he didn't think she trusted him with her daughter. Which wasn't true at all.

She knew to the very marrow of her bones he'd never intentionally hurt her baby.

Faith broke their connection by placing a tiny palm on Cole's cheek and turning his head toward her. "Can I ride the pony, too?"

"One thing at a time, Faith Marie." The ponies were separate from the petting zoo. "The ponies will wait until Mommy gets back." Dani glanced at Cole and caught his look of surprise. "Be sure to take pictures."

"I will." He grinned. "Come on, munchkin."

Setting Faith on her feet, he clasped her hand and led her toward the enclosure gate. "Has your mom ever told you how smart goats are? They're smarter than mean old trolls."

"I know that story. Billy goats..." Faith's chatter faded as the man at the gate waved them through.

Dani waited for the fear to come. She'd let her daughter go off and have fun with Cole without thoroughly analyzing the pros and cons, without considering how it would affect tomorrow, next week and Faith's teenage years.

Slowly she turned and headed for popcorn and lemonade. Any minute regret and worry would rise to claim her, haunt her for not taking the time to make a proper decision.

But wonder of wonders, she made it all the way to the snack booth and back without falling apart. She chose a bench that allowed her to see into the petting enclosure and sat.

Eating popcorn and sipping lemonade, she watched Faith and Cole huddled over a soft bundle of white fur. He helped her hold the tiny bunny and pet it gently. Not always an easy chore with an overeager three-year-old.

But with his gentle guidance, the bunny was as safe in her hands as she was in his.

Sighing, she let the weight of the impulsive decision fade away. Maybe there was a lesson for her here—that even though she was alone and totally responsible for her daughter's health and well-being, not every decision had to be a massive debate. Maybe sometimes she could just go with the moment.

And trust in an unexpected ally.

One thing for sure, there was a whole lot more to Cole Sullivan than a captivating smile and laid-back attitude. From the seriousness at christening classes to the vulnerable flashes of emotion she'd seen, and his pride and love in what he'd created here at Sullivan's, she realized the charming facade he showed the world hid a depth of character most people never saw. He even had his family fooled, which was amazing considering how close they were.

She'd have preferred to remain ignorant herself. She'd had a hard enough time resisting him when she'd thought him charming but shallow. As an honorable, responsible adult he'd be devastating.

CHAPTER SIX

COLE PULLED his Ford 150 pickup into one of the few subdivisions in Paradise Pines. He didn't care for the sameness of the homes, the sense of being one of many. But no doubt more would follow; few could afford to build on their own these days.

He found his destination and parked under the shade of an old oak tree. Climbing from the truck, he admired the view.

What a lovely picture mother and child made fussing in their small front yard. Faith pranced around in black pants and tiny black boots, her long-sleeved sweater in trademark pink, and two pink polka-dot ribbons tamed her dark hair into ponytails. In contrast her mother wore a faded University of Phoenix sweater shirt and torn jeans. A piece of the same polka-dot ribbon attempted—and failed—to contain the mass of sleek auburn tresses. Beautiful, both of them.

When he reached the driveway, and picket fence, he came to a dead stop, his heart stuttering as he viewed the yard in the full light of day. Here was a surprise and an unexpected delight. She'd created a garden fit for a princess.

Borders of verbena in waves of lavender to deep purple framed a lawn still green and lush for this late in the year. Slate pavers led the way to the corner away from the driveway and the shade of the house to a water fountain topped by a fairy happily gurgling amidst gladioli, towering black-eyed Susans, and some hearty and cheerful dahlias. Between the house and the water feature, a bougainvillea bower sheltered a patio swing.

Lovely, fanciful and full of color, perfect for a three-year-old. And for Dani it was an obvious labor of love.

Now he understood Gram's question. He did admire a woman who knew her way around a garden.

"There, how does that look?" Dani adjusted the medium-size pumpkin on the porch a smidge to the left. She looked over her shoulder at Faith. "What do you think?"

Faith jumped up and down and clapped her hands. "We got the bestest pumpkins ever."

"The best," Dani corrected as she stood back and surveyed the results of their efforts.

"Yep, the bestest."

Dani laughed, wrapped her arms around her baby and kissed the top of her head. Then she admired their work. They stood in the small yard facing the shallow porch that ran half the length of the house.

On the ground and first step were seven apple-size pumpkins with rosy cheeks, big red noses and soft felt caps. On the porch the medium-size pumpkin also had rosy cheeks, a smaller nose formed by the pumpkin itself, and wore a black wig, banded in red. Around the base was a high white collar. Eight pumpkins in all.

"Snow White and the Seven Dwarfs, not your usual Halloween jack-o'-lantern, but effective," he drawled.

"Cole!" Faith broke free and ran toward him.

He reached over the picket fence and snatched her into his arms.

"What are you doing here?" she asked, all smiles.

"Good question." Dani strolled over to release the catch on the gate.

He shifted Faith to pull an envelope from a pocket in his black leather jacket. "Pictures from Saturday."

"Right. Come on in." She waved at the pumpkins. "You like the pumpkins?"

"Original. I see you used paint instead of carving."

"I got the idea from one of the craft booths at Sullivan's on Saturday. A paintbrush is a lot less dangerous than a knife when working with a three-year-old." She held out her hand. "Can I see the pictures?"

"Sure." He handed them over.

"We're having a picnic in the yard," Faith said from her perch in Cole's arms. "You want to picnic, too?"

"Oh, well." He looked at Dani. "Don't you think we should ask your mom first?"

A small frown pulled her little brows together. "She might say no."

He arched an eyebrow at Dani.

She stood, hands on her hips, surveying the two of them. A soft blush colored her cheeks, but was it due to pleasure, annoyance, or just the chill in the air?

He waited, realizing he'd hoped for such an invitation. But he didn't flirt, didn't flash his crooked grin—it just felt wrong. He couldn't be casual with these two; they'd lost too much, known too much hurt for a carefree relationship.

Dani deserved respect, Faith protection. Actually they deserved a whole lot more. And for the first time, he wasn't running in the other direction.

"You're welcome on one condition: no political talk at the picnic."

Now he grinned. "Sold. I don't care if we never talk politics." There was the Lord's honest truth. He detested the fact his was the voice opposing hers. Which reminded him he still needed to invite her to participate in the debate. Tough. It could wait until after the picnic.

She cocked her head, probed him with eyes steady and clear. "You almost say that like you mean it."

"I do. Politics have never been my thing. Politicians want everyone to love them, and to have that you have to please people. The problem is when you try to please too many people, you end up pleasing no one."

"Yeah, that's politics all right. But we're not talking politics right now. We're having a picnic."

"Picnic, yeah!" Faith called from high in Cole's arms. "Can I have a cookie, Mommy?"

"After you eat your sandwich, yes."

"Can I have two cookies?"

Laughing gray eyes met his as Dani reached for her daughter. "There's my little bargainer. I think we need to save some cookies for your guest, don't you?"

"You made lots of cookies, Mommy. Cole can have two, too."

"Let's have our sandwiches first." Dani led the way inside the house.

Though small, the open floor plan made the most of the living room, dining room and kitchen combo. Cole admired the color scheme of amber and brown with bursts of red. It suited her, solid and calm with passionate depths.

He watched her put the picnic together with Faith's help and soon they were returning outdoors, the backyard this time. Here Dani kept it simple, a green expanse of lawn off a covered patio. A few potted plants provided interest.

Faith raced to a play set with a swing and a slide. She climbed on to a swing.

The front was a place to dream, the back a place to play. Both were evidence of Dani's total devotion to her daughter. She mourned the loss of her husband, Faith's father, worried she wasn't doing enough, but she shouldn't fear. Love lived in this house, in this yard. And she was stronger than she thought.

"Push me, Cole," Faith demanded.

"Faith," Dani admonished.

"Please, Cole, will you push me?"

"Better." Dani bypassed the table on the patio to spread a blanket on the grass. She glanced at him. "Do you mind pushing her? I want to throw together a couple of more sandwiches. Do you prefer turkey or tuna?"

"Turkey." He shrugged out of his leather jacket and slung it over a patio chair. "And I was already on my way."

"Thanks." Her gray gaze caressed her daughter before returning to him. "I'll save you in a few minutes."

"Hey, Faith's my girl. Take your time."

Already turning to head into the kitchen, she stopped and shook a finger at him. "Not funny."

He laughed and winked, and then went to push the princess.

Dani was such a good mother that watching her and Faith together sometimes made his throat tighten and his heart constrict. Dani made him remember how it felt to be loved, which threw him, because he was a man with a lot of love in his life.

He knew from Samantha that two years had passed since Dani lost her husband. But from the way she had closed the door on him the other night clearly she wasn't ready for a new relationship. Plus he saw how it hurt her to see Faith seeking a daddy figure.

Then again, Dani didn't kiss like a woman clinging to the ghost of her husband.

Maybe the two weren't related. More than once Dani had mentioned difficulties in making decisions. If she was overanalyzing every thought and deed, then he could see the problem.

It was one thing to accept the natural process of moving on with your life, and another to consciously decide to put the man you loved, the father of your child, behind you so you could find happiness with someone new. Especially when your daughter had already made the leap and you were trying to hold on to his memory for her.

Stepping behind Faith, he gave her a big push, smiling when she shrieked with joy.

"Higher," she called, lifting her face to the wind she created with each pass of the swing.

No complications or communication problems here. The daughter knew exactly what she wanted and wasn't afraid to ask for it.

Maybe he and Dani should take a lesson from Faith, and go after what they wanted.

What they wanted?

Was he crazy? Was he suddenly thinking of picket fences and ready-made families? Exactly when had he gone off his rocker?

And why wasn't he headed for the nearest exit?

All he knew was being here felt right. The constriction around his heart filled him with a warmth he wasn't ready to let go of.

Her gaze on the view out the kitchen window, Dani slathered mayo on bread and then layered on turkey, lettuce and tomatoes.

She found it hard to believe Cole Sullivan was in her backyard. They were worlds apart, yet there he stood, patiently pushing her daughter on the swing. Not once had he looked up to see if she'd finished and would soon rescue him.

Her and her bright ideas. What was she supposed to talk to him about now that she'd forbidden discussion of the election and all things political?

She laughed to herself. Who was she kidding? Through the window she heard Faith chattering away. Dani and Cole would be lucky to get a word in edgewise.

Watching man and child, she experienced the oddest feeling of tranquility. He appeared to genuinely enjoy Faith's company and Faith thrived under his attention.

Even as Dani worried about his presence building up unrealistic expectations in Faith, Cole kept slipping past Dani's guard.

His potential to hurt Faith was huge. If Dani stopped and thought about it, no way would letting the two of them spend time together pass her exhausting decision-making process. Pretty much a given she'd say no.

So why was Dani skipping the process?

Hearing the trill of Faith's giggles, seeing the joy and animation on her little face, Dani had her answer.

Faith's happiness rated as Dani's number-one priority, and Cole made Faith happy. For the first time in a long time, Dani let that be enough. He'd proved he cared for Faith by adhering to Dani's ban of his company. And it hadn't really made a difference, except Faith got mad at Dani.

Until he betrayed the trust he'd earned, the ban was gone for good.

Of course life was never that easy, and Faith had her own agenda.

Once Dani had organized the food on the blanket, she leaned back on her hands and called out, "Food's ready."

A moment later Cole carried an upside-down and protesting Faith toward the blanket.

"We can play again after we eat." He told her as he set her on her feet next to the blanket.

"Promise?" she demanded.

"I promise." He held up a hand as if swearing an oath, not that Faith understood what the gesture meant.

Still she nodded, happy to have his word.

She plopped down next to Dani and leaned back on her hands, mimicking Dani. She grinned.

"I'm hungry. Can I have a cookie?"

"Uh." Dani made a point of rolling her eyes. "What do you think?"

Faith sighed. "I think I have to eat my sandwich first."

"That's right."

They both looked up to see a home-baked chocolate-chip cookie disappearing into Cole's mouth. He froze, got a deer-caught-in-the-headlights look on his face.

"Sorry," he said around a mouthful of cookie.

"Uh-oh, Mommy." Faith giggled. "Cole was bad."

"Cole is company. He doesn't know our rules. We'll cut him some slack this time."

He swallowed. "Thanks."

The three of them dug into the sandwiches and fruit, making their way to the cookies. Dani expected the conversation to be stilted; instead she laughed more than she had in forever.

Faith's latest thing was knock-knock jokes. She brought a new one home from preschool every time she went. Of course she often got them wrong. Which didn't matter, as Cole, being the next best thing to a kid himself, knew them all and more. They played off each other perfectly. And when she went off on a story or two about her classmates, Cole listened intently and asked all the right questions.

At some point Faith climbed into Cole's lap. Dani should have been expecting it, but the fun they were having distracted her.

"Cole." Faith tipped back her head to look up at him. "Do you ever want to be a daddy?"

His dark eyebrows flew up and his gaze collided with Dani's. She blinked and offered a small shrug. If he meant to hang around, he'd better be ready for the tough questions.

His innate charm saved him. "It seems to me your mama already has the best little girl ever, but someday I'll have kids."

She sighed.

"I hope you'll be their friend."

That perked her up. "I want to be their friend. You will be the bestest daddy ever."

"I'm going to try." His long, blunt fingers dug into her ribs, tickling her. Laughing, she wiggled this way then that, trying to escape his fingers.

"Didn't you have some drawings you wanted to show me?" he asked.

"Yeah." She hopped to her feet. "They're beau-ti-ful." She swung to Dani. "Mommy, can I show him my pictures."

Faith loved to draw and Dani hung all her pictures on a bulletin board in her bedroom. Not one of the drawings made sense without Faith's interpretation, but Dani loved them anyway. She knew the mess Faith would make taking down the pictures, but shrugged.

"Sure, baby. Be careful not to tear them."

"I will." Faith raced into the house, leaving Dani alone with Cole.

She should have known better than to doubt him. He hadn't charmed women the better part of his life without learning how to counter an awkward moment.

He showed he'd listened, addressed the question in a global manner, and then used his questioner's own interests to distract her from the original query.

Very effective.

"So you do want kids someday?" she asked.

"Sure. I like the little guys and I think I'd make a good dad."

She angled her head, considering him. Yeah, she did, too. "Are you planning to have a wife, too, or just a few of the little guys?"

He shot her a mock glare. "Of course I plan to have a wife. I know how the whole family unit works."

"Do you? Then you know it takes some serious stick-to-it-iveness."

He met her gaze straight on. "Contrary to popular opinion, I have been in a few long-term relationships."

"Really? How long? When?"

An arched eyebrow berated her for the rapid-fire interrogation. Surprisingly, he answered. "I was with the same girl most of my junior and senior years in college. And a few years ago I was in a relationship for over a year."

"So what happened?"

"What do mean? Nothing happened."

"So why didn't you settle down with one of them, start a family?"

He rolled his shoulders, obviously ill at ease with the direction the conversation had taken. "I wasn't feeling it. I liked both ladies—a lot—but not enough to build a family on. I didn't love them, but I didn't like hurting them either. Now I keep it casual and short-term. We have some good times and no one gets hurt."

Dani studied him with narrowed eyes. Really? He expected her to buy a noble excuse for playing the field?

She found it convenient, but...unpracticed. Being in foster care taught a kid to read people early in life. From the sincerity in his eyes and the lack of tension on his face, Cole truly believed in his love-'em-and-leave-'em system.

Which made her wonder why he kept spending time with her. She had a child—already too attached to the man—and even before she had married and had Faith, Dani hadn't done short and sweet.

Was she high maintenance? No, she didn't think so, but commitment, yeah, she wanted to know the man was planning to make an effort. She'd had too many people come and go in her life for her to risk her heart easily. And she preferred no affection to the false affection of instant sex.

"If you don't stick around and work at a relationship, how will you know when you've found the one?"

He looked around the yard, and she

thought *evasion*, but he kept looking until he landed on her, sweeping his blue gaze over her hair until she felt the need to tug at her unruly ponytail. Then that intense gaze moved down, measuring the cling of her sweatshirt to her breasts and lower to the valley and curves of her body. When his eyes met hers, it took a blink to clear the fog from her mind. He made no effort to hide the awareness, the desire, in his.

"Oh, I'll know. It won't be work, for one thing. And being with her won't be something I can walk away from. That hasn't happened yet."

"Sounds like you have it all figured out."

"It's working so far. Actually, this conversation reminds me I wanted to ask you for a favor. I want to have a thing—you know, a brunch or buffet thing, at my place, to celebrate the christening. Since I'm not currently seeing anyone, I wondered if you'd help me put something together."

"Oh, but—" Dani sat up straight "—Samantha has done so much for me, I wanted to have something here."

His assessing gaze rolled around the yard again. "This is nice, but we're a big crew when the whole family gets together. With kids, cousins and friends, it would be a crush out here. Plus in late October the weather can be unpredictable. My place is bigger inside and out."

She frowned, reluctant to give up her plans. "It wasn't too crowded at Gram's at Sunday dinner."

"Sweetheart, that was a fraction of the people Sami will want at the celebration."

Resigned, she asked, "What kind of help are you looking for?"

"Menu, decorations, preparations."

"In other words, all of it?"

He grinned. "Pretty much. But I'm not looking for you to cook. I thought we'd cater, and I'm willing to help. Whatever you need. If I can't do it, I'll find someone who can. What do you say?"

"Okay," she agreed, because she really wanted the day to be special for Samantha and her family. "It's only a couple of weeks away. I need to see your place soon so I can start making plans."

"Sure. We can go over there now."

"Oh." Dani hesitated, not sure she was ready to invade the intimacy of Cole's home.

The two weeks decided her. With campaigning added to her regular schedule, time flew by these days.

"Cole, I got 'em all." Faith erupted from the house, waving her drawings in her hands, colorful pom-poms of artistic effort.

Cole winced and amended. "Actually, we can go right after the viewing."

Dani nodded and reached for the used paper plates. "Just enough time for me to clean up."

CHAPTER SEVEN

RIDING SHOTGUN in the front of Cole's truck, Dani wondered about his home. No doubt it had a fabulous garden, or maybe not. Maybe after working with plants all day, he kept his yard simple and clean.

To her dismay she was alone with the man. Faith had fallen asleep in his lap, so Dani called the teenager next door to come over and babysit.

They rode in silence, not surprising. The easiness of it did throw her. Whenever she spent time in his company, her awareness of him hummed beneath her skin. It buzzed there now, a faint reminder she was alive and a woman. But mostly it felt good just to ride along in the peace of early evening.

He headed in the general direction of the nursery, turning a mile before the entrance.

People tended to pick homes near where they worked for convenience's sake. When she had worked as a nurse in Phoenix, she'd lived in a condo two blocks from the hospital.

After he turned, they began to wind up the side of a hill, threading through spearing pines, weaving steadily in the direction of the nursery.

"The nursery must be right in your backyard," she said as they made another turn.

"Close," he confirmed, and pulled into a long driveway, facing a large, sprawling house with rolling decks and a wall of windows. A spectacular view of the valley spread out before them. And Dani knew when she stood on the deck she'd be overlooking the nursery below.

He owned the house on the hill.

But wow. He'd said his place was big; understatement. The downstairs alone could swallow her little home, yard and all, and have room left over for dessert. And she couldn't get over the view.

"My God, this is beautiful," she breathed, hearing the awe in her voice and not caring. The setting sun reflected off low-riding clouds. Pink and orange blazed across the sky, casting the hills and valleys of Paradise Pines in rosy hues. Heaven must look a lot like this.

"I want to see everything."

"Come on, then." Cole stood there holding out a hand.

She blinked in surprise. "Where did you come from?"

"Yeah, it still does that to me, too." Wrapping an arm around her waist, he lifted her from the seat and set her on her feet. "Welcome to my home." Taking her hand, he led her forward. "Come on, I'll show you around and then we can make plans."

Dani cherished her little place. It was hers, a safe haven for her to raise Faith. And she'd give it up in a heartbeat for Cole's house on the hill. The open floor plan, the gourmet kitchen, the way the tall windows brought the outside indoors—she loved it all. The house spoke to her on an elemental level.

She couldn't wait to play house.

Maybe she shouldn't assist Cole after all. He already got to her more than she found comfortable. Now that she knew his master suite had a private deck complete with a spa, she may not be able to resist him.

His large, comfortable furnishings were

dark brown and gold with touches of navy blue and a soft buttery-cream. A large island separated the family room from the kitchen, which was fashioned in dark cabinets, stainless-steel appliances and granite counters in rich amber.

Sighing, she watched him make coffee: decaf, though he'd made a face. Time to get down to business. She tapped a pen on the pad she'd taken from her purse.

"What type of food did you want to have?"

"My brothers are meat eaters, so I thought prime rib or ribs."

She shook her head. "This is a christening. Ribs are too messy. Prime rib is better." She made a note.

"I thought we could rent tables, set them up on the decks. And I want real tablecloths. This should be a classy event for them."

Dani saw the day forming as they talked. This was so much better than she could have done alone. For all their differences they worked well together, quickly making plans for the special day.

And she'd only hesitated for a moment at his casual use of the word "we."

* * *

As much as the sunsets were one of the things Cole loved most about his home, tonight it had paled in comparison to the woman basking in its glow. How stunning she'd looked bathed in the glorious reds and magenta of the fast-fading sun. Her auburn hair had darkened but was lit up with fiery highlights, the rosy glow of her skin, the sheer wonder in her wide silver eyes.

He wanted to taste the wine-red of her lips, change the flush in her cheeks to internal heat.

May as well forget it, though. His campaign committee was pushing for an answer to the debate question. Once Dani heard the proposal, he wasn't likely to be her favorite person. Probably not even in the top ten.

For sure she wouldn't want to be locking lips with him.

When she started making noises about heading home, he knew he'd delayed as long as possible.

Trying for a positive tone, he dove into the deep end.

"How would you like to participate in a debate? Have a chance to get the specifics of your museum/garden plans in front of an audience."

Immediately she straightened in her chair. Her shoulders went up and back and excitement lent a spark to her silver eyes.

"A public debate? That would be great."

He literally saw her mind begin to buzz with the possibilities as she pulled her notebook back out of her purse.

"When? Where?"

He cleared his throat; this was where things were going to head south. "At the Paradise Pines Small Business League."

She deflated before his eyes, stuffed the notebook back in her purse. "The Small Business League? Thanks but no thanks."

"It's a chance to get your issues out there, to be heard by an influential element of the community."

"Please, this is the group that had the plans drawn up for the sports complex." She singed him with a chiding glare, her disappointment clear. "I wouldn't be heard, I'd be dismissed. And I've already had plenty of that without magnifying it times thirty. Is your faction so threatened by mine it can't entertain the idea of a real debate?"

"This would be a real debate."

She rolled her eyes. "Right. We both know

it's a bone being tossed to the underdogs. You're hoping we'll stand down if we feel we've been heard. Guess what? We have our own campaign to reach the public. We don't need your pseudo debate."

Legs crossed, arms closed in front of her, she kicked one sandal-shod foot, toes painted the palest of pinks. She studied him as if he were one giant puzzle.

"If you don't like politics and you don't want to win, why are you running? Why agree to the appointment in the first place?"

"I didn't agree to the politics, I agreed to help out. Our last mayor died, heart attack. The board fractured, they needed someone to bring them together."

"And they chose you?"

He shrugged. "People like me."

"You don't appear to have been suffering this last year."

"I'm a social guy, so the public forum doesn't bother me. Hard decisions have to be made, that doesn't bother me either. You gather your information and make the decision."

"So what's the problem?"

Giving himself a moment to gather his thoughts, Cole fetched the coffeepot, filled her cup and then his. He rarely revealed his deep thoughts, or talked about his feelings or what motivated him. He preferred to skim the surface. Somehow that wasn't enough with Dani. Not when she looked at him with those genuine gray eyes. There was nothing false about Dani and she deserved to know what she was getting into.

"There's no downtime," he said, reclaiming his seat next to her. "Whenever, wherever, you're always on. Everyone has their own agenda and they all want something from you. I don't mind getting my hands dirty, but I prefer they be in the earth when I do."

Her eyes narrowed and he fought not to squirm. He swore she saw clear through him to all those places he kept carefully hidden, some even from himself.

"They all thought they could sway you, get you to do what they wanted," she guessed.

It had to be a guess. How did she do that, see so deep into him? It was disconcerting and oddly flattering. She cared or she wouldn't make the effort.

"They were wrong." Still it galled that they'd thought he was so easy.

"It's your own fault, you know. If you acted more seriously, they'd take you more seriously."

His head reared back as if he'd taken one on the chin—it stung just as bad. "Do you really want to get into shrink talk? You really want to cast some stones?"

She stiffened at his tone, and her chin shot up.

"I wasn't casting stones, I was stating a fact. It bothers you when people dismiss you, but you let them believe you don't care. You can't have it both ways."

"People see me as I want them to see me. It's nobody's business if I keep part of myself private. If you're serious about this election, you should learn to do the same."

"Why? Are you going to reveal me as a fraud? Tell everyone I'm afraid of my own shadow? That I worry over every decision to the point of pain? Are you going to tell them I'm a coward and that I have to force myself to let my daughter out of my sight each day?"

"Dani," he whispered. Shocked and concerned, he covered her hand with his.

"Oh, God." She stopped her rant, ducking her head to hide her features.

For a moment silence reigned over the table, their wounds raw and exposed.

Avoiding his gaze, she reached for her coffee. Inhaling a deep breath, she released it slowly over the steaming brew. "So much for decaf. I could have enjoyed the high-octane stuff."

Cole took that to mean she didn't expect to sleep much after her mini meltdown. The woman needed to give herself a break.

Before he could say so, she jutted out her stubborn chin again and soldiered on.

"Go ahead, do your worst," she challenged. "Because I don't expect to win. I just want our proposal to get a fair hearing."

After a moment, he blinked, all signs of vulnerability disguised by harsh control hidden behind his customary facade. She may see him better than a lot of people, but she didn't know him, not if she believed he'd throw her to the lions.

And she didn't know herself either.

"You think any of that makes you weak? You lost a husband in a violent act and he became a hero in the eyes of the world.

That's pretty hard to live up to. Everyone's scared of something, it's how you handle the fear that defines you. Have you fallen apart? No. You moved your daughter to a new state and started a new business. That takes guts and planning. And being a single parent isn't easy. I lost my parents when I was eleven. I know what it's like to feel an emptiness inside you think will never go away. To spend each day wondering what might happen next, and would anyone else be taken from you."

"But it's been two years." Chewing her bottom lip, she repeated what so many had told her. "I should be over it by now."

"There's no getting over it." He leaned forward, stared into silver pools of despair. "You just learn to cope, and you're doing that."

"You don't know." She bowed her head.

"What's to know? You may be scared, but you're making major decisions. And you're building a life for yourself and Faith. You're a fierce mama bear but you don't project all your worry and fear on Faith. You're the hero. If anyone can get this town to listen to the museum proposal, it's you."

She slowly lifted her head, her hand a

balled fist on the granite counter. The hope in her eyes nearly broke his heart.

"Do you really believe that? That I'm strong?"

"I do," he said easily. "And you better be prepared," he cautioned. "Because your beauty shop brigade could push you all the way into the mayor's seat."

"That won't happen." She shook her head, her rueful tone a clear indication she had her composure back. "We both know the museum proposal doesn't stand a chance. And most of my brigade—as you call them—knows that. But connecting citizens of Paradise Pines through history, tradition and education is important and shouldn't be dismissed as laughable. We just want respect."

"So you'll agree to the debate, then?"

"That's a no."

He sighed. "Will you tell your people to start cooking again?"

"Certainly." She agreed too easily, all signs of tears gone. "As soon as you're ready for a real debate."

He had given her the keys to his house.

Dani sighed and shook the thought away.

She refused to let the man disrupt her concentration.

Forcing herself to focus, she smiled at the young mother in her chair and asked what she wanted done today.

But after she helped her client into a robe and sat her back for a wash and condition, the woman fell silent and Dani's thoughts began to wander.

Cole Sullivan was a dangerous man. His charming smile and easygoing attitude hid a man of unrelenting persistence, surprising responsibility and devastating vulnerability capable of sliding through the best of defenses.

He threatened everything she'd built for herself and Faith here in Paradise Pines. Dani needed to keep her distance and keep her cool.

Easier said than done when the cosmos and the good citizens of Paradise Pines kept throwing them together. Or so it seemed.

Just when Dani had convinced herself she had a handle on her emotions, he managed to weaken her resolve with random acts of intimacy. And he always knew exactly what would get to her.

Like giving her the keys to his home.

With the christening only three days away

she'd already bought new outfits for Faith and herself and had the accessories all planned out. However, much still needed to be done in preparation for the celebration brunch. With the ceremony at ten in the morning, she wanted everything ready the night before so she could concentrate on getting herself and Faith to the church on time.

Before her client arrived, Dani had just finished a phone call with the caterer, who wanted to view the space today for prep and presentation purposes. And the cleaning service would be out tomorrow. Which left Saturday for delivery of the rental furniture and any decorating she intended to do.

With the nursery so busy and being tied up in meetings for the upcoming Harvest Fair and Dance, Cole had given her the keys to help organize and supervise the comings and goings. Between running her shop and campaigning with special interest groups, coordinating the party made her life a real juggling act.

Samantha's appreciation and excitement made the effort worth it. She'd been so thrilled Cole and Dani were hosting the brunch she'd practically been in tears.

Shutting off the water, she wrapped the woman's hair in a lavender towel and led the way back to her station.

"All right, I've had it." A pretty blonde in a purple velour sweat suit barged through the front door of the shop. "Dani, we have to do something. I'm sick of my husband's cooking and he hasn't even noticed the house going to dust."

"I know." A brunette swiveled in her stylist's seat to chime in. "I can barely stand my place and all my husband does is rave about how happy he is I've stopped vacuuming during his games."

"Well, we've had some success with our presentations at the Senior Center, the Knitting Guild and the Golf and Reel Club." Dani tried to offset the obvious frustration. "Plus we have school meetings set at the elementary and middle schools. I don't think we need to continue—"

"Oh, yes, we do. If you're going to say we can stop the home campaign, forget it," a third voice broke in with her opinion. "This is personal for me, I want my husband to acknowledge my right to vote as I please."

"And we're not getting any public support either. Their offer of a debate was a mediocre attempt to allay our right to a public forum."

At that point everyone began to speak at once, talking about their personal experiences and complaining about lack of appreciation from their significant others.

Dani focused on the woman in her chair, giving her concentration to the cut. She knew the fight at home was important to these women, but she couldn't connect with them on that level and she wondered if they weren't taking things too far.

A few minutes later, Mrs. Day, Lydia and Gram came through the door. Good. Dani appreciated the help. Strategies began flying, but it soon became clear what the next step needed to be.

"No sex," Gram stated baldly. "You want a man's attention, sex is the answer."

A resounding silence fell over the room. Even the snip of scissors ceased as Gram voiced what had been on everyone's mind but nobody had wanted to be the first to say.

"That would get my husband's attention."

"Mine, too."

"You don't think that's too extreme?"

Mrs. Day fussed. "It seems to me these lessons in listening are costing us women more than the men."

All eyes turned to the gray-haired woman. She shrugged, an unrepentant twinkle in her eyes. "A woman has needs."

Heads bobbed in agreement.

Dani carefully set her curling iron aside and moved into the middle of the room.

"I don't currently have a man in my life." She obstinately pushed aside the picture of Cole that flashed before her mind's eye. "So I can't make the decision. Plus, we'll have to get the agreement of the others in the 'Make Them Listen' campaign, but it starts here, with you. Is this a step we want to take?"

Silence descended again as the women looked from one to the next. Slowly heads began to bob.

"Sacrifice is necessary in any war," Mrs. Day conceded.

"We have to." The blonde spoke for the group. "It's a matter of principle."

CHAPTER EIGHT

COLE TOSSED his jacket over a chair back and, when he didn't see Dani in the house, wandered out to the deck. Deep violet silhouetted the horizon, the last dramatic skyscape of the sinking sun.

He found Dani dozing in a lounger as if she'd fallen asleep watching the brilliant sunset. Like a bee to pollen, he was drawn to her presence. Curled on her side, she had one hand tucked under her cheek, and her lustrous hair covered her shoulder like a fiery cloak. Light from the living room fell over her in a golden glow.

God, it felt good to come home to a welcoming light and a beautiful woman. Warmth bloomed from the center of his chest and spread outward. Looking at her made his heart swell.

This week had been both exhilarating and a nightmare. He'd been so busy he wanted nothing more than to lie down beside her and sleep for the next twelve hours. But working with her on the party, having someone to help, someone with brains, humor, creativity and an indomitable spirit had helped tremendously. They'd made a great team and pulled off a difficult week with remarkable results.

She was so hard on herself. She didn't see the brave, talented, together woman he did. She worried over being too careful, struggled over her decisions. So what? It meant she cared; it meant Faith was getting the proper attention and Dani's shop was flourishing.

Life was tough, but she was handling it. And looking down at the dark smudge of her lashes on creamy smooth skin, he wanted nothing more than to make it easier for her.

Not that she'd let him. *Obstinate* should be her middle name.

Unable to resist, he sat next to her, leaned forward and softly kissed her cheek to wake her up.

"Hmm." She shifted, opened sleepy eyes, closed them again and snuggled into the hand cupping her cheek.

"Hey, beautiful, how you doing?"

Her whole body rose and settled in a sigh. "Tired."

"I can see that." He used his free hand to gently tuck her hair behind one delicate ear. "The place looks great."

"Yes," she responded without opening her eyes.

"They took care of you at the nursery? You got everything you wanted?"

"Yes."

Her breathy answers changed what he felt, from emotional warmth to physical heat. He leaned closer so his words moved the hair at her temples. She smelled divine, like sunshine, jasmine and woman.

"You have everything you need for you and Faith for the morning?"

Another body sigh. "Yes."

He nearly groaned at the feel of his arm cushioned between the softness of her breasts. She was so sweet, so luscious, so accommodating he couldn't help himself.

"You want to take this upstairs where we can be more comfortable?"

Her eyes flew open and for just a second he saw raw desire in the mystical depths. He was too close to miss it, too attentive to misread the stark longing for anything but the true passion it was.

"No." In a blink the attraction disappeared, her customary caution falling into place.

"Then we'll stay here." Not willing to lose the moment, he claimed her mouth, drawing the desire back to the surface. She melted against him, sinking into the kiss.

When her mouth opened under his, he groaned. She tasted better than she smelled, oh so sweet. Wanting more, he deepened the embrace, pulling her closer and inviting her to open to the demanding heat of his tongue.

With a soft moan she retreated. Licking her lips, she lifted his hand from her curves to her mouth, where she bit the pad of his thumb harder than she needed to.

"Ouch." He grimaced, but the bite only ignited his fire more. Rather than pull away, he traced her lips with his damp thumb.

"You're a wicked, wicked man, Cole Sullivan," she stated, her voice husky from sleep and passion.

"Why," he challenged with a smile, "because I want to do wicked things to your lovely body?"

"Yes." Breathy. "I mean no. Wait…yes." She shook her finger at him and then pushed him away. "Wicked. I have to get home. What time is it?"

"Just after seven." He rose and helped her to her feet. "You're running scared," he tossed out, teasing, but serious, too.

"Pretty much," she agreed, making no attempt to hide the fact. She bent and lifted some rolled-up papers that had fallen to the ground.

Holding them up, she said, "You want to explain these?"

Frowning, he took the roll and recognized some sketches he'd been playing with. "These are nothing."

"They're plans for a sports complex, but different than the one proposed. This one has a memorial fountain with a floral surround including six historical markers and a statue of Anderson. It's not a museum or botanical garden, but it's a big step up from a plaque on the side of the snack bar."

"These are just some ideas I was messing with. I dropped the soccer fields, because I figured it wouldn't take much to convert the current sports field for soccer. They currently play at the high school, and Alex mentioned how torn up the football field has gotten."

"It's brilliant. Needing less land for the new sports complex would leave funds available for converting the current field and re-sodding the football field. Win, win, win for the sports crowds, and the fountain is a nod to the museum/garden supporters. Shows someone listened. That's important. When are you going to show them to the public?"

He shook his head. "I can't. As the current mayor and a candidate, it would be a conflict of interest."

"No," she protested. "Don't tell me that. What about the original plans?"

"Palmer hired someone to draw them up for the town meeting. I wasn't involved. I never meant anyone to see these. At least not until after the election and then only if I lose. As a city official, it's against my fiduciary duty to profit from city funds."

"But—"

"Dani, I can't show anyone these plans, and you can't tell anyone. Promise me you'll forget you saw these."

Reluctantly she nodded.

She pulled her jacket tighter around herself

and checked her watch. "I should go. It's not too late. I can still make it home before Faith goes to bed."

He moved toward her, and she moved away. Avoiding his eyes, she ran her gaze over the deck, checking her work.

"I guess I've done all I can for now. The caterer's crew will put the tablecloths on the tables out here tomorrow when they get here, hunter-green with white china and napkins. And we have market umbrellas to put up if it's hotter than predicted." She stopped babbling to look up at him. "It does look good, right?"

He knew she'd had the nursery send up a dozen three-foot-high topiary plants. To each planter she'd added an airy white bow, a classy tribute to celebrate the event. Scattered throughout the house and deck, they brought unity to the areas, which would give the guests a sense of being involved whether inside or out. White rose centerpieces were scheduled to be delivered in the morning.

"It's perfect. Thanks for all the help."

"It was a team effort."

"True, but let's be honest, you handled the bulk of the work, and it's going to be great."

"As long as Samantha is happy," she said around a huge yawn. "Sorry."

"Not a problem. Sami will be ecstatic." He followed her inside. He wasn't ready to say good-night. "You want me to drive you home?"

"No, I'm fine. Besides I need my car to get to the church in the morning."

"I can pick you and Faith up in the morning. And your car will be here when you're ready to leave tomorrow."

"Tempting, but no." She picked up her purse and found her keys. After crossing to the door, she stopped and turned to face him. Her slumberous gaze almost brought him to his knees. "I'm not sure I can trust myself to be alone with you."

The door closed softly behind her.

Cole plopped down on the sofa. Oh, God. He'd fallen in love with that strong, gorgeous, vulnerable, annoying, elusive woman.

Sunday morning dawned bright and sunny, fluffy clouds floating in a blue sky. The perfect day for a blessing. Standing in the church with the jewel refractions of the stunning stained glass window raining down upon the christening party, Dani savored the beauty of the moment.

As she held eight-month-old Jake with Cole at her side, his hand warm in the small of her back, surrounded by the love and support of his friends and family, she reflected she'd rarely known a more powerful moment.

"That cinnamon color looks stunning with your hair," Samantha whispered to Dani. Lovely in a violet wraparound dress, she fingered the cap sleeve of Dani's sweater dress. "We are a pretty crowd. Have you met Rick and Rett yet?"

Before she had a chance to respond, Cole shifted so he joined the conversation, his hand sliding from her back to her waist. She wondered if the gesture appeared as proprietary as it felt. She should protest, but today she was coupled with Cole and she found she didn't want to fight it. It may be wrong, but it felt right and she decided just to enjoy what the day brought.

"Samantha, my darling," he said smoothly, "you look too young to be the mother of three boys."

"You lie, but I love you for it." Obviously

pleased, Samantha gave him a hug, wiggling her eyebrows at Dani as she did so, a clear sign his hold on Dani spoke as loud as she feared. "I was just telling Dani what a good-looking crowd we make. It was a struggle getting the boys into their suits, but worth the effort."

"They are handsome." Dani admired the boys in their mini suits. All the men were suited up, including Cole. And he looked fine, straight, tall and distinguished, shoulders wide as a house. She glanced up at him. "All the Sullivan men look handsome today."

He smiled, his head lowering toward her.

Dani caught her breath. Did he intend to kiss her here in church? Again? He wouldn't dare! Both appalled and thrilled, she couldn't bring herself to pull away.

His lips warmed the skin of her temple. "You're the loveliest woman in the room."

Her pent-up breath escaped in a rush of happiness. "Thank you."

"Good morning, Sullivans," Father Paul greeted the group. "Are we ready to begin the blessing?"

The ceremony began and Dani and Cole stepped up to the baptismal fountain at the priest's direction. Faith, clutching the hem of Dani's skirt, moved with them.

The priest took them through the blessing. Dani and Cole said their lines, candles were lit, the baby anointed. Jake behaved beautifully, fussing only a bit when the father dribbled the water over his forehead.

As she held Jake over the fountain, she felt a tug on her skirt.

"I can't see," Faith complained.

"I'll get her." Cole immediately came to the rescue. "Come here, sweetie." He lifted Faith into his arms and she stayed there for the rest of the ceremony.

Dani loved the weight of little Jake in her arms. She almost didn't want to give him back, but everyone wanted time with the guest of honor so she handed him off to his father with an exchange of hugs.

And then Faith was there wanting to know if she had got the water poured on her when she was a baby, and four-year-old Gabe came running over to whisper in Faith's ear and no time existed for wistful sighs.

The brunch at Cole's proved a raving success. The weather played nice, warm enough to make the use of the umbrellas practical, but a nice breeze kept people from crowding indoors where it was cooler but there was less seating for meals. The caterer, a gal new to the area whom Mattie had recommended, got so many requests for introductions, she finally joined the party while her crew handled the service. She took over in the kitchen again when it was time for cake.

Best of all Samantha and Alex just relaxed and enjoyed the day. Laughter and happy voices filled the house with a festive vibe.

In his element as host, Cole wandered from group to group, charming and teasing with equal measure, flirting with the ladies, young and old, and kicking it with the dudes from little Jake to tottering great-uncle Bill.

Whenever Cole moved from one group to the next, he touched base with Dani in between. Literally touched her, a simple cup of her elbow, an arm around her waist or shoulders, or that warm hand in the small of her back. He was constantly putting his hands on her.

And she liked it.

Guests began to depart and, as the crowd thinned out, Dani started collecting used cups and plates. As she went through the living room, Gram stopped her.

"Dani, dear, put that down and come sit with me. You've done enough for today and Cole told me the catering included cleanup."

"Don't mind if I do." With a sigh from the feet up, Dani sat down next to Gram on the living room sofa. She set her collection of cups and plates on the coffee table to be taken to the kitchen later. "I hope you've enjoyed the day."

"I have. It's been lovely. And it's such a treat to be able to sit back and enjoy." Gram patted Dani's hand. "I know Cole appreciates your help."

"He could have handled it alone, but I was happy to do it for Samantha's sake. She's done so much to help me since I moved to town."

"Don't minimize your contribution, Dani. I see your influence everywhere." Gram sipped her coffee. "Not least of which on Cole."

Dani frowned. "What do you mean?"

"I've watched him with you today. It's obvious he's smitten."

Dani scolded herself for the excited buzz Gram's assessment sent tingling down her spine.

Stopping short of a full eye roll, Dani sent

Gram a wry glance. "Cole is a flirt, Mrs. Sullivan. We both know he doesn't mean anything by it."

"Please call me Gram." The older woman set her cup on the coffee table. "I know my grandson, Dani. I've never seen him so possessive of a woman before."

Dani had no business being pleased by the statement. "It's just the proximity. Between the christening classes and working together this week, we've been in each other's pockets."

"The way he looks at you, the way he returns to your side, I think it's more than that." Concern touched the blue eyes, but was the emotion for Dani or Cole? "Does that scare you?"

Yes, more than anything in a long time. And that said a lot. Not that she could confess such a thing to his grandmother.

"I'm sure you're wrong. Cole doesn't do serious."

"He doesn't do jealous either, but he hasn't let Rick or Rett within ten feet of you all day."

"I don't understand."

"Come, dear. Samantha's matchmaking has been less than subtle and Cole is taking no chances of one of his brothers catching your eye."

"Oh, but…" Could Gram be right, could Cole have feelings for Dani?

Or was his grandmother simply seeing what she wanted to see? She'd made no effort to disguise her desire for him to find someone to settle down and start a family with.

Dani looked for Cole and saw him outside on the deck. He stood leaning back against the railing, Faith asleep in his arms, as he talked to the infamous twins. Rick and Rett had the Sullivan dark hair, blue eyes and good looks, only amped up a notch. Their features were more defined, bringing their male beauty into sharp detail.

Was it true Cole had been sabotaging introductions to the two men?

Dani found it hard to believe.

Even if he were interested in her, his confidence should handle an introduction to his brothers. But as she watched, one of the twins pointed inside to where she sat with Gram. Immediately Cole stood to attention though his features remained casual. She saw his lips moving and after a moment, he shifted Faith in his arms so he could reach inside his pants pocket. He pulled out keys and handed them to one of the twins. The two men walked down and off the deck and Cole came inside.

He caught her eye and motioned he was taking Faith upstairs. Dani nodded and then turned to find Gram watching the whole flow of events.

"Coincidence," Dani said.

"You're too smart to believe that," Gram chided her. "I'm sure you've heard it from plenty of well-meaning people, but I'm not going to tell you it's time to move on with your life. We all grieve at our own pace. I've been a widow for over twenty-five years, so I know some men are difficult to forget."

"It's not just that."

"Of course not. It's never just one thing. And you're doing the best you can. But this is my grandson, whom I love very much. For all his charming ways, he's more vulnerable than he appears." Gram squeezed Dani's hand. "Cole doesn't give his heart easily. All I ask is you don't hurt him."

Wow, that was a switch. Worried about her own chances for hurt, Dani never considered Cole might suffer from their association.

All day she'd been playing hostess to his host. And this morning in the church Dani had realized she'd been envisioning a family for her and Faith, complete with a daddy and a new baby.

That was so not where she was.

Obviously Samantha's matchmaking and Faith's talk of a new daddy had reached Dani on a subliminal level, leaving her open to romantic suggestions.

As the mother, it was her job to help Faith get over her daddy fixation, not let Faith drag Dani into her fantasy.

Obviously, Samantha and Faith were bad influences, and Dani'd be smart to stay far, far away from both of them.

And even farther away from Cole.

Upstairs Cole laid Faith in his bed and carefully covered her with a throw. Brushing back a dark curl, he felt a swell of love for the child. She'd stolen his heart even before her mother had.

He'd almost gotten used to the idea of loving Dani. At first he'd fought it, convinced himself it was heartburn, a hallucination or sheer exhaustion. The flimsy excuses changed nothing, his feelings never changed.

He loved Dani.

And he loved having mother and daughter here in his home. It felt right having Dani as his hostess, and his heart expanded when little Faith climbed into his arms and fell asleep. The trust and affection of the gesture touched him deeply.

Tonight confirmed for him that they belonged together as a family. Now he just needed to convince her of the fact.

Leaving a light burning in the adjoining bathroom, the hall door ajar, he headed back downstairs. He couldn't afford to be gone long or the twins would get to Dani. No need to tempt fate.

Halloween followed close on the heels of the christening. Faith, dressed as the Little Mermaid, went trick-or-treating with the Sullivan boys.

Dani strolled the streets of her neighborhood with Samantha and Alex while the kids ran from house to house. The streets had been closed to nonresident traffic, so the subdivision was flooded with kids.

Her party stopped at a house decorated with a large air balloon of a Frankenstein monster and the kids tromped up to the door. Dani casually surveyed the street behind them. Keeping her tone oh so nonchalant, she finally asked the question on her mind.

"Did you say Cole was going to join the trick-or-treating? Should we wait for him before going too far?"

"No," Alex responded. "We saw him when we went by the nursery, and he said he wouldn't be able to make it. One of his workers called in sick so he's driving the tractor for the hayride."

"Oh." Let down, she hid her disappointment with a smile. "I bet it's quite a party out there."

"Yeah, it always is. And Cole stays open as long as people keep coming by."

"Yes, he would." Dani easily saw Cole sticking it out so the kids could have fun. He was built that way.

She'd deliberately kept her distance in the days since the christening and it surprised her how much she missed seeing him, talking to him, laughing with him.

Faith and the boys came tripping down the walk and the group moved on to the next house. As the kids repeated the process, Samantha vented about the upcoming Harvest Dance.

"The dance is only two days away and all the plans are falling apart." Samantha rubbed her hands together to generate heat. The temperature had dropped as a cold front went through the valley.

"Sami, the plans are fine. Nobody is as organized as you. Give it a chance, everything will fall into place."

Samantha sent Dani a frazzled glare before turning to her husband. "Alex, sweetheart, Dani and I are going to walk ahead a bit. Can you handle the kids for a few minutes?" At his assent Samantha pulled Dani into the middle of the street.

"I'll be so glad when this election is over," Samantha lamented. "It's the darn sex campaign. Tempers are frayed."

"It's not a sex campaign," Dani protested. "It's meant to make the men and women supporting the sports complex listen to a view other than their own. We had to anticipate the men would get grouchy."

Samantha snorted. "It's not just the men. Sure they snarl occasionally, but mostly they stay out of the way of the catfights. The point is tempers are short. The Harvest Dance is the biggest deal in town, which means the women were already jockeying for position on the committee. Now women who barely get along are frustrated and fighting for power."

"Put them all on decorations," Dani suggested. "Let them put their frustrations into physical labor."

"Very funny. I can hold it together long enough to get the event off the ground, but it's not going to be very festive when half the town isn't talking to the other half."

Dani linked her arm through Sami's. "It'll be fine. Music soothes the savage breast. Once the band starts, everyone will get into the spirit of things."

"I hope so. Otherwise, it's going to be a very long night."

CHAPTER NINE

"I TOLD you so." Samantha nervously drummed her fingers on the table as she looked around Sampson Hall.

The community center had been turned into a harvest bower with strategically placed white trellises festooned with fall foliage and strung with hundreds of tiny white and orange lights. A haunting love ballad floated on the air courtesy of a live band.

"It's magical, Sami," Dani complimented her. "You and your frustrated committee did a fabulous job."

"You're laughing, but nobody is dancing. You promised me they'd dance."

"It's early yet," Dani tried to reassure her friend even though the feel of the room was thick with tension. "Once people have tried the appetizers and had a drink, they'll settle down to dance."

"It'll be fine, honey." Alex settled a hand over Samantha's restless fingers. "And if it's not, it won't be your fault. You did your part, and Dani's right—the place looks great."

"Well this place is like a morgue." Cole pulled the chair out next to Dani and sat. He laid his arm across the back of her chair and leaned so close Dani inhaled the spicy scent of his cologne. "The work of your beauty shop brigade if I'm not mistaken."

He wore another suit, this one a dark navy that was a near match for her ankle-length midnight-blue halter dress. The color of the suit did marvelous things for his blue eyes. Sitting next to each other, they were going to look like a couple.

How much of a coincidence was that? Glancing at Samantha, Dani truly wondered.

"No need to exaggerate." She shifted in her seat and sent him a telling stare trying to telegraph the message he needed to remove his arm. She liked it too much, and talk about shouting *couple*.

"No. See, see." Samantha actually brightened at Cole's disparaging comments.

"Finally, someone who understands. It's a disaster waiting to happen, am I right?" she demanded of her brother-in-law.

Cole's shrug embodied careless sympathy. "When you're right, you're right."

Dani dug her elbow into his ribs. "You're not helping." Lord, forget the appetizers, the man smelled good enough to eat.

"Dani." Samantha stopped just short of a wail. "We have to do something. You have to do something."

"Me?" Dani protested. "It was Gram's idea." She blew out a breath in exasperation. She'd known this idea was going to bite her in the tush before it ran its course.

Looking for inspiration for a fast fix, she spied Cole's brothers Brock and Ford arriving with their wives. The foursome stopped to say hello to Gram, who was acting as part of the town council welcoming committee.

"There's no need to panic." Dani relaxed a little. "People are still arriving. Nobody hops right out on the dance floor. It's going to be fine."

The four Sullivans reached the table and the men held chairs for their wives before taking seats.

"Wow, it's dead in here tonight," Rachel said as she set a tiny white purse on the table, a perfect accessory for the off-the-shoulder white sheath dress she wore.

"Dani!" Samantha groaned.

Dani stopped herself from banging her head on the table.

"Oops, my bad," Rachel apologized. "Obviously a sore subject."

"Sami's worried nobody's going to dance, but it's early yet, right?" Dani held her breath, needing the reassurance almost as badly as Samantha at this point. Dani disliked seeing her friend so upset.

"Not really." Jesse shook her head, her dark hair moving softly over the shoulders of her little black dress. "This crowd likes to dance. As soon as the music starts they're usually on the floor."

"All my hard work," Samantha fretted, "and it's going to bomb."

"Okay, enough." Dani turned to Cole, found him far too close but didn't let it stop her. "I need you to agree to a debate. The election is Tuesday. We can do this. Tomorrow. My supporters will be able to enjoy themselves if they think they're going to be heard."

He hesitated.

"You owe me," she told him. "For keeping your plans a secret."

His gaze ran over her and she knew he was thinking about his campaign committee and the grief they were going to give him if he agreed. "Okay. Where?"

"Here. We'll do it outside on the steps."

He nodded, and for one brief moment she felt the heat of his thumb rubbing over her bare shoulder. His touch soothed her in ways she didn't really understand but appreciated just the same.

"I'll be here," he said. "We'll get J.T., too, make it fair all around."

"Thank you." He really was a decent guy. With his agreement, she addressed the others at the table. "Okay, there are eight of us. When the next slow song starts, we're all going to take to the floor to start the dancing. Then after a minute, we split up and ask someone from the audience to join us. Pass the word about the debate. Tonight is for fun, tomorrow we can think about the election again."

"Brilliant." Samantha reached for Dani's hand and squeezed. "It just may work."

"It's worth a try," Brock agreed, and he

lifted Jesse's fingers to his mouth for a kiss. "But once you get the men and women talking again, you may lose them to something more than the dancing."

"I don't care," Samantha declared. "At least they'll go away happy. And have good memories of the dance."

"All right, let's go, then." Ford stood and pulled Rachel to her feet. "I'll talk to the band, make this happen."

"Yeah, let's go make friends." Rachel pushed back her chair.

"You guys are great. Thanks." Dani's throat closed up at the unquestioning show of support.

"Hey, we all want to have fun—" Brock winked "—before moving on to something more."

Heat rose in Dani's cheeks, but she grinned through the blush. She shook her finger at him. "No disappearing until the dance is declared a success."

Brock cocked an eyebrow.

Alex bumped his brother's shoulder. "You'll know when that is, because we'll be gone." He took Samantha's hand and led her onto the floor as the music started.

Dani let out a slow breath. This might

actually work. And she had her debate, a win-win for everyone. Well, except for Cole's campaign committee, but they deserved any grief they suffered.

"Dani?"

She looked up. Cole stood to her right, his hand extended for hers.

"Shall we dance?"

Automatically, instinctively, she hesitated.

"It was your idea," he reminded her.

"Oh, but…if we split up…"

"I insist." He stole her hand, pulled her gently to her feet. "Consider it the price of my cooperation."

"Okay." She sighed softly as her body settled against his taller, harder one. "But only the one dance."

He moved her easily through a turn, his arm strong around her, his hand warm and steady on her lower back. Oh, yeah, the man could dance.

And this was why her mind balked, because her body didn't. Once in his arms she wanted to snuggle, to burrow in and absorb his heat, his strength, his sheer maleness.

In his arms the world went away and it was just him, just her, and pure sensation.

But that was a lie her body believed. In her head she knew better, knew it was never that simple. And you could never rely on anyone but yourself.

"Time to split up," he whispered near her ear. "I'll take my dance later." He sent her into a controlled twirl where she ended with her back to his front.

"I—I said only one." She struggled to get the words out.

"This isn't a full dance. Doesn't count." With that he spun her out to the full span of their joined arms then bowed and released her. With an easy smile he walked to Lydia from the sheriff's office and plied his charm.

Scrambling for composure, Dani spied J.T. and made for his table. Smiling, she asked his wife, "Do you mind if I borrow J.T. for a moment? I have some good news."

Well into the evening, Dani sank back into her seat with a small moan of relief. She savored the moment alone, having just said goodbye to Samantha and Alex, who were taking Gram home.

Dani had been on her feet almost constantly since that first dance. The citizens of Paradise

Pines had embraced her brilliant plan and the dance had taken on a life of its own.

Jesse said it, the people liked to dance. And not just with their men. They often grabbed a girlfriend, or three, and hit the floor. Not so much the guys, but they were happy to gather in the corner and talk sports in between bouts of being dragged to the dance floor.

Dani had danced with all the Sullivans, including Gram. The women were energetic, the men smooth, and Gram could really shake it.

The only one to keep his distance was Cole. Beast. He had threatened her with another dance and then never came to claim it so the tension grew with each new song. He'd come for her when he was ready. In the meantime she'd pretend dread, when in fact anticipation zinged through her blood.

He'd been on the dance floor almost as much as she had, with his sisters-in-law, Gram, Gram's friends, Mrs. Day—the list went on and on. But, other than family, he danced with no one under fifty.

He was approached by more than one woman on the prowl and he smiled and chatted, but it never went further than conversation.

He may not have claimed his dance, but his eyes touched her often. She felt the weight of his gaze, the heat of it. He knew exactly who she'd danced with, had followed her moves, the sway of her hips, the lift of her arms, the swing of her breasts.

His concentrated attention made her wonder if Gram didn't know her grandson better than Dani thought. Could Gram be right, could Cole have feelings for Dani?

For some reason the thought didn't scare her as much tonight as it had on the night of the christening. Did that mean she liked the idea or she'd just gotten used to it?

The music slowed, softened, and the female singer stepped up to the microphone. Cole appeared at Dani's elbow. Without a word he held out his hand and she took it.

As the singer seduced the audience, Cole pulled Dani close. There were no showy moves this time, no turns or twirls. He simply held her in his arms and moved to the sexy ballad.

And Dani surrendered. She gave up thought, worries, inhibitions. She sank into him, her head on his shoulder, right arm around his waist. Linking her fingers with his, she let him lead her into a melodic journey of sensual motion.

"You take my breath away," he said, his lips a tickling caress on her ear. "These lights bring out the fiery highlights in your hair."

"Hmm. I planned that with Samantha."

He chuckled. "Just as you wore that dress because it brings out the gray in your eyes."

"Shh. You'll give away all my secrets."

Being in his arms changed the way the world worked. It narrowed and heightened at the same time. Everyone disappeared but him, yet her senses imploded, making everything around her come alive.

The song, one of her favorites, eclipsed all other sound, while against her chest she felt the pounding of his heart, the rhythm a match for hers. She savored the smooth texture of his shirt under her cheek and hand, and the leashed male strength below both. The spicy scent of his aftershave mixed with the homey touch of coffee and the freshness of pine when the breeze blew just right.

He surrounded her but she had no sense of being trapped. He invigorated her, challenged her to do more, be more, risk more.

The song ended, the music moving to

something more upbeat, and still he held her, his lead barely more than a sensual sway. And though she knew they received more than a few odd or speculative glances, she let him. She closed her eyes and drifted.

Finally he stepped back and said, "I'll take you home."

She nodded then remembered. She'd come with Samantha and Alex after dropping Faith off for a sleepover at Gram's house. A set of teenage twins were hired to watch the whole Sullivan brood while the adults enjoyed the evening. And Brock and Jesse, who lived in San Diego, were staying over so they'd be there to help in the morning. Faith had been invited to join them.

"That's all right, your brothers are giving me a ride to Gram's."

"They're not ready to leave yet." He nodded toward the two couples enjoying the music and each other. "You'll be more comfortable with me."

She chewed her bottom lip. Decisions, decisions. Be an intrusive fifth wheel or ride alone with the temptation that was Cole Sullivan. Fatigue decided her and he read the answer in her eyes.

"Grab my jacket and whatever you have. I'll let my brothers know and meet you at the door."

A short time later she sat in his truck cab, the weight of his jacket warm around her shoulders. Blessed silence settled between them and Dani closed her eyes, just for a moment. She felt his hand curl around hers and didn't know anything else until the door next to her opened.

She blinked, focused on Cole's beautiful blue eyes. "Hey."

"Hey. You're home."

"Home." She yawned. "Right. That was fast." She swung her legs around and slid from the cab into his arms. "Hmm, so warm."

"Come on, sweetheart, let's get you inside." Tucking her under his arm, he led her toward the house.

The icy crispness in the air had woken Dani somewhat by the time they reached her front door. It wasn't until she turned to thank him that she remembered. "Wait. My car is at Gram's."

"Don't worry. I'll pick you up in the morning and take you over to get it. You fell asleep. I thought it best."

Okay, that annoyed her. But it also touched her. He'd been a good sport tonight, helping to kick-start the dance, agreeing to the public debate, keeping his distance. All right, that was stretching it, but for the most part he'd behaved himself.

She opened the door then impulsively went up on her toes to kiss his cheek. "Thank you for your help. I had a good time tonight."

"It's about to get better." He leaned close, stopping short of her lips.

Sweet harvest peaches, what was he waiting for? A protest? For her to pull back? What? She wanted him to close the distance, to take her to wonderland. When he didn't come to her, she moved the necessary centimeter to reach him. Which was what he wanted all along.

And it was so worth it. Her lips on his, her arm around his neck, she sank into the kiss.

Once she surrendered and he had her mouth under his, he took over, claiming her with bold thrusts of his tongue. Oh, she liked that dance. Angling her head, she showed him how much and earned a low moan from him. Or was that her?

His hands left her face to trace her curves

and she arched into him, telling him with her body she longed for more of his touch. He complied, pushing his jacket from her shoulders and running his fingers along the flesh left bare by her halter neckline. Heat flared from nerve to nerve, warming her insides, melting her bones, leaving her weak in the knees.

Too much, too fast.

She pulled back a scant two inches, rested her forehead on his shoulder. His touch sent her into such turmoil. With arousal at fever pitch it was difficult to think, but instincts died hard. Desire clashed with self-preservation, putting mind and body at odds.

She should send him away but couldn't make her arms release him. It felt too good to be held.

"How come you didn't dance with anyone tonight?"

"You must not have been paying attention." He feathered his fingers through her hair. "I danced a lot."

"Yeah, with matrons and married ladies. Why didn't you dance with anyone young, pretty and unattached?"

"Because the only woman I was interested in held me to one dance."

"Oh." The tension drained from her shoulders and she relaxed against him again. A small smile tugged at the corner of her mouth. He always knew what to say to get to her. "Really?"

"Really." He lifted her chin on a knuckle so she was forced to look into his eyes.

The raw passion caused the breath to catch in the back of her throat, but the sincerity and caring prompted her to take his hand and lead him inside.

He allowed her only a step before he pulled her to a stop. "Are you sure?"

"Yes. Stay." When he looked at her, she felt he really saw her, Dani, the woman, not the mother, businesswoman or candidate. He made her feel beautiful, desirable, alive. And she wanted more. She wanted it all.

Above all, she wanted Cole.

And she got all of him. Once he had her assurances, he gave her no chance to change her mind, taking her deep with the next kiss, heightening her arousal with skill and patience while maneuvering her to the bedroom.

Lying in Cole's arms, Dani savored the closeness she'd missed for so long.

He burrowed his nose against her temple. "Now that's what I call dancing."

She kissed his chest. "I'll say this, you sure know how to tango."

He rolled so they were nose-to-nose, her feet tangled around his shins. His gaze probed hers. "Are you okay?"

She smiled and lightly traced his jaw. "Better than okay."

Everyone made him out as just a charmer, yet he was so much more than that. He was loyal and smart and altruistic. He gave far more than he took. And he cared. More than she did.

More than she could.

"No." He kissed her, trying to bring her back to the moment. "Stay with me."

"I want to."

"Then do." He linked his fingers with hers, brought them to his mouth for a little nibble. "Let's deal with this. Tell me about him."

She rubbed the sole of her foot over his hair-roughened calf as she gathered her thoughts. "He was the home I never had. He promised he'd always be there for me. But he lied."

"Dani." Cole cupped her cheek, his touch demanding she look at him. "It wasn't his fault he was taken from you."

"I know," she said with stark honesty. "It was my fault."

"No."

"Yes. I sent him to the store. He would never have been there, but I sent him for coffee and diapers."

"That's just life."

"No, you don't understand. I didn't think. I didn't weigh the consequences of my decision. Didn't consider what was more important, having coffee in the morning or my husband's life."

"Oh, sweetheart." Compassion lit his eyes. "And you've been second-guessing every decision since then."

"Second-, third- and fourth-guessing." It shamed her to confess it, but she'd already revealed her weakness to him once before.

"It's a wonder you let Faith out of your sight."

"For the first six months I didn't. It's still hard. Worse, once I make a decision, half the time I wish I could call it back. Like running for mayor. Thank God there's no chance I'll win, because I'm woefully unqualified to run the town."

"It would probably be the best thing for you. Force you to get over this part of the grieving process and move forward."

She stiffened. "What do you mean?"

"You're still in the denial phase. Once you accept—"

"I know Kevin is dead." She pulled away and, sitting up, used the comforter to cover herself. "I live with the fact every day."

"You mean you beat yourself up every day." Cole pushed up to sit against the headboard, the sheet pooled in his lap. "It wasn't your fault. It wasn't his. Certainly it wasn't your decision that killed him. The man with the gun killed him. Kevin just happened to be in the wrong place at the wrong time."

"Because of me."

"That might be why he went, but it's not why he died. Did you tell him what store to go to? Did you have control of the traffic or the number of people in line at the store? A lot of factors enter into why he was in that spot at that time, most of them having nothing to do with you."

She chewed her bottom lip, letting his words roll around in her head. She wasn't ready to say he was right, but he did have points she hadn't considered before. Things she needed to think about. Because, Lord, she was tired of being uncertain.

"Dani." Cole swept his thumb over her tortured bottom lip, soothing the swollen skin. "I know it's hard to disassociate yourself from what happened, but consider this: you don't blame Faith because she needed diapers."

She blinked at him, struck by his words. Of course she had never blamed her innocent baby. Faith's needs had nothing to do with the drugged-up thug with a gun. And Dani understood that was the point Cole wanted her to reach for herself.

It was something to think about, because the Lord knew she needed to get her mind to a better place, not only for herself but for Faith, too.

Moving to Paradise Pines had made such a difference. It had given her control of her life again, forced decisions on her.

Even running for mayor had helped. Maybe because so many decisions were needed so quickly it was impossible for her to agonize over every one.

And then there was Cole, who made her feel rather than think. He defied all her good intentions, her cautious planning, her fretful denials.

Thank God.

"Hey, beautiful." Cole trailed a finger down the naked length of her back. "I didn't mean to make you sad."

She shivered at the sensual touch. It was just what she needed to bring her back to the moment.

Half turning to him, she eyed him through her lashes. He was sprawled in splendid male dominance, confident yet compassionate, demanding but giving. It stunned her to see him in her bed.

"I can't remember the last time I was this happy."

His self-satisfied grin made her pulse trip again.

"I should send you home. I have a debate tomorrow, I need to be fresh."

"You want me to leave?" The smiled dimmed, his disappointment clear and immensely flattering. Yet his gaze held no censure, no reproach.

"I didn't say that." She crawled up the bed to him. "Why don't I see how happy I can make you?"

CHAPTER TEN

THE NEXT AFTERNOON Dani opened her shop and took the Closed for Debate sign from the window. She stepped aside and let her unofficial campaign committee parade through the door.

It was a relief to sit at her station and kick off her shoes. Gram settled in the chair next to Dani. She glanced at the somber older woman, and then looked around the room at the slumped shoulders and subdued expressions. She'd let her team down.

"Tell me again why we fought so hard for a debate?" She threw the question out, knowing it was the one on everyone's mind.

"We wanted to be heard," someone muttered.

She closed her eyes then opened them to gauge reactions. "Tell me truthfully, was that as big a debacle as I think it was or am I being overly sensitive?"

"Oh, it was bad," Mrs. Day confirmed. "But you kept your cool. You were informed and intelligent and you tried to keep on topic."

"Yeah, Dani," one of the young wives said. "You did a real good job of hyping the museum/garden proposal and the need to keep tradition and history alive in the community."

"Not that anyone heard her." Lydia cut to the chase in her blunt manner. "Heck, for that matter they didn't hear Cole either. So in that regard we didn't lose ground." She sent Dani a baffled glance. "Or we wouldn't have if you hadn't started campaigning for him."

Dani's cheeks burned.

"To be fair, he did a good job of campaigning for her, too," Gram interjected on a wry note.

"We needed more preparation," Samantha said, "and a better format. I thought you were brilliant to open the questions to the public. It was an opportunity to directly address their concerns."

"Yeah, except their concerns had more to do with my social life than community affairs," Dani lamented.

"Oh, they seemed very interested in community affairs," Lydia said, tongue in cheek. "Yours."

"Oh, my gosh." Dani had to fight to hold her chin up high. "I've never been so embarrassed in my entire life."

"I thought it was so romantic how Cole kept coming to your rescue," a dark haired woman said. "Nobody can blow hot air better than that man."

Dani shot forward in her seat. "That's not true. Cole is honest and sincere. He came up with those great modifications to the sports complex, adding the statue of Anderson along with the fountain and historical plagues. Cole is a well-respected businessman who's put his own interests aside for the past year to help run this town—"

"All true," Gram cut into Dani's defense of her grandson. "And he blusters better than anyone I know. He pulled out all the guns today. I think the crowd's biggest disappointment was they went away with no new information about the two of you."

"Yeah." Samantha pouted. "I'm one of that crowd." *Call me*, she mouthed to Dani.

Dani fanned herself; her stylist's chair had

just become the hot seat. "That's because there's nothing to say."

"Uh-huh, that's not what my cousin says." The young wife shook her finger. "She saw Cole's truck outside your place when she went out for the paper this morning."

"Oh." Small towns, you had to love them. Or move. And Dani was here to stay. "He dropped me off last night—"

"Dani." Lydia stopped her. "It's all right. We're happy if you're ready to welcome someone into your life. And Cole is a scoundrel, but we love him. And he's a free agent. Plus you're right, he stepped up for the town."

"Well, we can honestly say we made history in Paradise Pines today," one of her more chipper supporters said. "It was our first public debate."

There were several hums of agreement.

"And probably our last," Mrs. Day avowed.

Everyone laughed.

"I can promise you it was my last," Dani stated with vehemence. "I'm sorry, ladies, but I'm pretty sure I won't be winning the election. And it's pretty much a given there will be no museum and botanical garden."

"We put up a good fight, that's what counts. The modifications Cole suggests for the sports complex sound pretty cool."

Dani winced. She'd gotten carried away in his defense and blown the secret about his plans. He'd immediately donated the plans to the city as an example of changes that could be made to better suit the needs of the city.

"Hey," the dark-haired gal piped up, "those plans prove they listened to us. We were heard after all."

A shout of approval went up.

"And the debate wasn't wasted. It saved the dance." The blonde wife chimed in. "Afterward, my husband apologized for being so high-handed. And we made up." She giggled. "Twice."

"Nice." Another woman nodded. "It was the same for me. My husband said he missed me so much we left the dance early, and he promised never to try to tell me how to vote ever again."

There were echoes of the same from all over the room and the mood changed, became downright cheerful. Dani began to feel better. They may not have won the war, but they'd definitely scored some victories.

Samantha wandered over and leaned against the counter behind Gram and Dani. "Well, it looks like the museum and garden are casualties of the battle."

"True," Gram agreed. "But the women wanted to be heard, to have their husbands respect their opinions. They've gotten both."

"I'm happy about that." Dani swirled her chair around to face the two women. "It means my running for office hasn't been a total bust. But it's a good thing I have no chance of winning, because I can never show my face in public again."

J.T. won the election.

Which was both a relief and unexpected.

Late on Tuesday night, long after the city election results were declared, Dani kissed Faith's cheek and tucked a blanket up around her shoulders. Surprisingly, the election results gave her mixed feelings. Sure, she was happy—she'd never really expected to win—but she also felt an odd sense of letdown. Not really disappointment, more the end of something special.

Running her fingers over the silky softness of Faith's hair, the feeling eased.

Nothing was more important than having time for her daughter.

Exhaustion from the long day started to drag on Dani. She quietly rose, set the nightlight and closed the door.

Tonight she'd turned the shop into election central, brought in food, sodas and a TV to watch the results trickle in. Despite the loss, the atmosphere had been one of a party. She and her supporters had found a victory they could accept and that's what they celebrated.

In her bathroom, Dani brushed her teeth. One thing she would keep from this whole experience were the friends she had made.

Before she stepped into the shower, a knock sounded at the door. Pulling her sweater back over her head, she wondered who was here so late, though in her gut she knew. With the election on top of them, she and Cole hadn't found a moment to be alone together since Saturday night after the dance.

The memory of being in his arms added zip to her steps.

Yep, Cole stood on her doorstep, bad-boy handsome in his black leather jacket. His crooked grin and the bottle of champagne in his arms told her he was as happy with tonight's results as she was.

He swooped in for a kiss so luscious it warmed her in the chill of the open doorway. When the caress ended they were inside.

"Hello," he said, his breath cool on her damp lips. "I've missed you."

"Me, too." She grinned, suddenly revitalized. "Congratulations on your loss."

His lips curled up. "You, too. I brought bubbly to celebrate."

"So I see."

"I borrowed a friend's car and parked a couple of houses down."

She groaned. "You heard about that?"

He nodded.

"I hope your friend's and my neighbor's reputations can handle it."

"There are three other cars just like it out there. Somebody would have to be looking for trouble to make something of it."

"Well, then." She kissed him softly. "I'll get some glasses."

He followed her to the kitchen with the champagne, and she directed him to the drawer for a corkscrew. With deft skill he popped the cork and bubbles foamed up and over the edge of the bottle. Watching Cole at work in her kitchen left Dani feeling as light and fizzy as the wine spilling into the glasses.

Taking his hand, she led Cole into the living room and snuggled into the corner of the couch with him. She clicked her glass against his. "Congratulations, J.T."

"Amen." Cole sipped. "He's a solid guy. Paradise Pines is in good hands."

"Hmm. I like his wife, too." Dani smiled as the wine tickled its way down her throat. "He stayed out of the endowment controversy, do you think that's what won it for him?"

"Maybe. The sports complex took the vote, but J.T. told me there were enough write-in comments for my compromise plans that he wants to see a formal proposal to present to the new board. And if they decide to use the donated plans, they'll hire my company to do the work."

"I'm so glad to hear that. I'm sorry I blew your secret. But I have to tell you, my supporters look on those plans as a victory for our side. You're brilliant." She kissed his cheek. "Thank you."

He cupped her cheek as he lowered his head and took her mouth. She moaned her pleasure at his sensual mastery as he sought the taste of her. When he lifted his head, she sighed and shifted, nipping his jaw lightly and then soothing the small bite with soft licks of her tongue.

He took her glass along with his and set both aside on the table then turned back to lie against her. Grinning, she looped her arms around his neck and pulled him the last few inches until they met mouth-to-mouth.

With soft murmurs and whispering sighs, he lavished praise on her, telling her how beautiful she was. She could live in this moment. Did live when so often she simply existed. Equally tender and demanding, he took her from languorous to satiated until she melted in his arms.

Sighing, he turned them so they were on their sides facing each other. "You make me wish the nights had more hours so I could hold you all the longer."

Eyes closed, she smiled. "Sweet-talker."

She felt his sudden stillness and opened her eyes to focus on his. The blue depths held a serious intensity.

"Just because it's sweet doesn't mean it's not true."

"I know." She traced his lips with a single finger.

"Yes," he agreed. "You've always seen me better than most."

"They've known you longer, believe the facade you've taught them to see."

He half smiled. "They should. Even I believe the charade most of the time. But not when I'm with you."

"It's not a charade," she protested. "It's who you are, and there's nothing wrong with being charming and friendly and funny, because you're also so much more than that. You're smart and talented, confident and caring."

"Stop. You make me sound like a Boy Scout. What I'm trying to say is it didn't matter what people thought of me until you came along. That was my first hint you were different than the other women in my life."

"I'm different?" she asked.

"Special," he confirmed, his gaze steady on hers. "Which you proved when you moved the rubber plant on my advice even after you threw me out of your shop. And I was a true goner once I saw your yard. Your garden is a fairyland for your daughter. And the backyard a safe haven for play. How could I not fall in love?"

"What?" Dani sat up and looked down at Cole. The world suddenly moved too fast. "You love my garden?" Surely that's what she'd heard.

"I love you." He grinned, dimple flashing, confident, sexy.

"Because of my garden." Her heart pounded out of control. She'd just gotten a reprieve from becoming an elected official; now Cole was declaring his affections. She couldn't think, couldn't juggle emotions fast enough in a spinning universe.

His avowal both elated and terrified her.

And typically he showed no hesitation.

"Partly. Mostly because you're resilient and brave, accepting and obstinate, incredibly gorgeous and a really good mother." He reached up, caught a tendril of hair hanging in her eyes, and tenderly tucked it behind her ear. "Let's give Faith her wish. Marry me."

She shook her finger at him. "That's not funny."

"It's not meant to be." He sat up, too, some of the joy fading from his features. "I'm serious."

"Cole." She picked up his hand, so strong yet capable of exquisite gentleness, just like the man. "We've barely got past being enemies."

"We've never been enemies, opponents sure, antagonistic maybe, but never enemies. I have too much respect for you."

"I respect you, too."

"No, don't do that." He stood and reached for his clothes. "Don't start pacifying me. Don't pretend what you don't feel."

"I'm not," she assured him, trying to think, to keep up with the deteriorating conversation. She knew he wanted more from her, expected a reciprocating statement, but he'd caught her off guard. "I do respect you. And…I care for you."

His face turned stony. "I love you."

"Cole, I'm sorry. I know you want more from me, but I haven't gotten that far. I've barely allowed myself to admit I want you. I need time."

"Sure." He stuffed his feet in his shoes and grabbed his jacket on the way to the door. "Take your time."

"Cole proposed?" Samantha eyed Dani through suspicious green eyes.

"Yes." Dani nodded. Just saying the words

out loud gave her a brain freeze. Yet at the same time her heart pounded, not with anxiety but with longing.

"As in marriage?" Samantha clarified.

"Yes," Dani confirmed, her gaze flicking to where Faith and Gabe played in the child's play area of Parkway Plaza. The inside mall was great for shopping therapy and Dani had dragged Samantha along with her. As they sat with bags at their feet and flavored coffees in their hands, Dani had confessed what was bothering her.

"But you haven't even had a real date yet."

"I know." Dani nodded and gestured at Samantha as if she'd made the very point Dani found so obvious. "Crazy, huh?"

"You're messing with me, aren't you?" Samantha demanded. "Teasing me because I want this so bad."

Dani frowned at her friend over a sip of coffee. Suspicion wasn't exactly the reaction she'd expected.

"Sami, focus. This isn't about you. Cole proposed and I don't know what to do."

"Hey, if you expect me to tell you to turn the man down, you're talking to the wrong woman."

"Sami."

"Okay, okay, let me refocus." Samantha took a deep breath, released it slowly and then turned toward Dani. "Cole proposed. Exactly what did he say? I take it this wasn't another fake proposal like he's done before?"

"No." How Dani wished he'd been playing. She'd hated the hurt on his face as he left her house last night. "He said I was special, that he loved me and we should give Faith her wish and get married."

"Hmm." Samantha pursed her lips. "Not the most romantic proposal, but including Faith shows he accepts she's part of the package. Was he at least down on one knee?"

"No, he was naked on my couch." Hearing the words escape, Dani quickly glanced around to make sure no kids were listening. She got a wink from a grandmother on the next bench over and her cheeks heated.

"Even better."

"Sami, be serious. I don't want to hurt Cole, but I don't want to get hurt either. I was feeling so adventurous to start a fling with him. I'm not sure I'm ready for more."

"Dani." Samantha patted Dani's knee, offering warmth and comfort. "I know how hard losing Kevin was for you. And I know your fear of loss goes deeper than that. You told me once that as a foster child you couldn't allow yourself to care about a new family because it hurt too much when you had to move on again. When you lost Kevin, you went back to that place."

Emotion swelled up in Dani's throat. Unable to speak, she simply nodded.

"Let me ask you a question. Do you regret the time you had with Kevin? Knowing the pain you'd suffer, would you change what you had with him?"

Oh, God, she covered her face with her hands. Her first instinct said yes, protect the heart. But that was totally defensive thinking. She spread her fingers to watch Faith seated next to Gabe in the little train, and knew she could never regret the union that brought her her baby. More, Dani had been happy with Kevin. She'd had her own home, her child, her man. Final answer, she couldn't regret her time with Kevin, not for her sake and not for Faith's.

She shook her head. "No. I loved my time with Kevin."

"I know you did," Samantha said softly. "And that's what you need to hold on to. The good is worth the bad. Next question, do you love Cole?"

Dani shook her head. "I don't know. It's so fast. And I've worried about how Faith will react to a relationship between us. What if it doesn't work out? Then I've hurt her, too."

"Stop." Holding up her hand, Samantha halted Dani's downward spiral. "Don't tell me what you think, tell me what you feel. What does your heart say?"

Her heart betrayed her. Her heart wanted Cole's arms around her; it wanted the laughter he brought to her home, and his help with Faith in the midst of a party. Her heart admired his loyalty, his vulnerability, and his love of the land and all things organic. Most of all her heart wanted to belong to him.

But she couldn't just say it. Couldn't just leap into love.

When she didn't answer, Samantha squeezed her hand. "Trust your heart, Dani. I did, and I've never looked back."

Dani shook her head. Because for every beat of her heart urging her to take a chance on love, her head pleaded with her to be cautious, to save them all from future pain.

"I can't deny Cole has pestered his way into my heart, but I can't trust my heart to keep me safe, to keep Faith safe. It's one thing not to regret having found and lost a loved one, and a whole other thing to welcome that pain back into your life when you're finally beginning to function again."

"But don't you understand, Dani, it's the risks that allow you to function. The one good thing about you running for mayor was it gave you a purpose beyond Faith to focus on. Since Kevin died, everything in your life is about providing for her—even your shop. The campaign was a risk but it brought you new friends, new drive, new life. Don't lose that forward momentum because you're afraid to take a chance."

Dani bit her tongue. Yes, her motives for running for mayor were to save her shop and to push herself beyond her comfort zone. And she was proud of her accomplishments. But had she grown enough to take this risk?

"Mama! Mama! Look at me," Faith called from the train. Dani smiled and waved. Next to her, Samantha did the same. The kids giggled. So happy, so carefree.

"I'm scared, Sami. What I feel for Cole is so much more intense than anything I've ever felt for anyone else. Kevin was comfortable—we meshed and never argued. We were friends first, and then lovers."

"And with Cole?"

"Cole comes across as mellow and charming." A smile tugged at the corner of Dani's mouth. "But he's a live wire. And, oh, God, he lights me up. He's so funny, so unpredictable. I never know what he's going to say. What he's going to do. Which drives me nuts, but it also makes me laugh.

"We're comfortable with each other, too. And we worked so well together on your brunch. He adores Faith. And, oh, mama, he's so hot."

"Sounds like you're in love."

Dani nodded. "And that's what scares me."

CHAPTER ELEVEN

"YOU ASKED HER to marry you?" Alex pushed his two-year-old on the swing set in his backyard.

"Yes." Cole shifted baby Jake against his shoulder to shield some of the pain of rejection from his brother. "And was royally dissed."

"At which point you took off?"

"Hey, not wanted, not staying."

"So she told you to hit the road."

"Not in so many words, but I got the message."

Reacting to the tension in Cole's voice, Jake stiffened his arms and pushed against Cole's shoulder. "Shh," he murmured to the baby, patting his back.

"Higher, Daddy," Seth demanded.

"What were her exact words?" Alex pushed harder while keeping a sharp eye on his son.

"She said she cared but needed time." The words came out hoarse, squeezed through the constriction in Cole's throat. He had bared his heart to her and the best she could give him was caring? Hell, you cared about your assistant, your neighbor, the postman. A lover warranted more than caring.

Didn't he?

Cole paced to the sandbox and back, admitting to himself it never had before.

"So you've been dating each other for a month? Two months? And you were pretty sure of her feelings—"

"I'm not sure you can classify any of our outings as actual dates."

Alex sent him a quick glance. "What about the kiss in church? You weren't seeing her then?"

"Not exactly. What?" He shrugged off his brother's censure. "It seemed like a good idea at the time."

"In front of Gram?"

Yeah, that hadn't gone over so good.

"Maybe I was subconsciously staking my claim. She's had me twisted up since the dinner where you asked us to be Jake's godparents."

"But you're sure she has feelings for you?"

"Yes. She would never have let me in her bed if she didn't love me. She just doesn't trust herself."

Alex stopped pushing Seth to stare at Cole in disgust. "You're nuts."

"Hey!"

"What do you expect?" Alex shook his head. "Even I can see Dani's been struggling with decisions, second-guessing herself a lot since she lost Kevin. Being a single parent isn't easy. I can tell you when I had Gabe on my own, I was a basket case, and that was only for a few days."

"She knows I love Faith," Cole protested.

"You're not getting it. Marriage is a big decision. Most people would consider it important and want to give it serious consideration. Dani isn't most people. You're just used to women falling at your feet, so you expected Dani to do the same."

"Okay, I get it." Got that he'd been a jerk.

"Do you? She lost someone she loved in an unexpected, violent act. That's a lot to recover from. She asked for time, I wouldn't call that a rejection."

"No?" He couldn't keep pain or hope from the word.

"No. I think you should slow down and give her the time she's asked for. And don't forget, the two of you are babysitting for us next weekend. You'll have two days to woo her."

Damn, everything Alex said rang true. Cole should have known better. Sure he'd been hurt when she didn't immediately declare her love, especially as he knew her feelings were there.

Of course Dani needed time to consider his proposal.

He had to have surprised her, because, hell, he'd surprised himself.

What scared him, absolutely terrified him, was that she might let her fears steal their future from them.

"Yeah, I have that to look forward to, two days of heaven or hell."

"Mama, are you going to stay at Aunt Sami's, too?" An excited Faith bounced on Dani's bed.

"Yes. I'm going to watch the boys while Sami and Alex go away for the weekend." Dani turned from her bureau in time to catch her overnight bag before it fell off the bed. "Hey, missy, stop that bouncing."

"Sorry, Mommy." Faith sat down on Dani's pillow. "I'm excited to stay at Gabe and Seth's."

"Yes, you are." Love flooded Dani and she smiled fondly at her daughter. "Did you pack your pajamas?"

Faith rocked back and forth on the pillow. "Yep. And my slippers. And Mr. Snuggle."

"Good girl."

"Gabe said Cole is staying with us, too. Will he be sleeping with you?"

The question threw Dani, partly because of the memories of being in his arms but mostly because of the source of the question.

"Cole is supposed to be spending the weekend with us. But no, we won't be sleeping together."

"Aunt Sami and Uncle Alex sleep together."

"Yes, but they're married."

"If you married Cole, you could sleep with him. Then you wouldn't have to sleep alone."

And there it was. Her little girl had a one-track mind. And the persistence of a bulldog.

Dani knew if she made a big deal of the question, Faith would make more of it than Dani had the heart to deal with. She ignored the Cole part of the equation. She'd assured

Samantha she could handle the boys on her own and Samantha could let Cole off the hook for the weekend, but Samantha said Alex insisted he'd feel better knowing Cole was there to help.

Dani thought she might hear from him, but he hadn't called her all week, except to leave a message on her home phone last night. He was taking Samantha to the airport Friday morning and the boys would be at Gram's, who had invited them for a stew dinner. He'd see her there when she got off work.

His lack of inflection was so unlike Cole. It hurt her to think of him hurting. But she didn't know if she had the strength to fix things.

"I won't be alone." Dani tickled Faith's toes, making her giggle. "I'll have you and Mr. Snuggles for company."

Faith's eyes got big. "No, Mommy. I want to sleep in Gabe's room."

"I'm not sure that's a good idea." Actually she was pretty sure nobody would get much sleep with that arrangement.

"Uh-huh. It's a really good idea."

Dani zipped up her bag. "We'll see. Go put your shoes on, we're ready to go."

Gram had made a wonderful stew, both warm and hearty on a cold November night. But best of all, her company over dinner helped to smooth over the awkwardness between Dani and Cole.

He was polite but distant, giving his attention to the kids, making them laugh when he got down on the floor to play.

Dani feared Gram might express her displeasure over Dani and Cole's aloofness with each other, but the older woman kept her peace.

All too soon the meal ended and they loaded the kids into the vehicles to head for Samantha's. Once there Cole carried Dani's and Faith's bags up to the master bedroom.

She was still removing coats and jackets when he came back down.

"Can we watch a movie, Cole?" Gabe yanked on Cole's hand. "Please."

"Yes. A movie." Faith hopped up and down. *"Tinkerbell,"* she demanded.

Gabe shook his head *"Transformers."*

Dani looked between the two. "If you can't agree—"

"Transformers."

"Tinkerbell."

The kids switched their choices at the

same time. Dani and Cole exchanged glances.

"Since Faith is your guest, how about we watch *Tinkerbell* tonight?" Cole rubbed Gabe's head. "And tomorrow night we can watch *Transformers*."

"Okay." Gabe smiled up at his uncle. "Come on, Faith, let's get the DVD. It's in my room."

The kids ran off and Dani nodded at Cole. "Well done."

"Thanks." He shrugged dismissively, but his eyes didn't meet hers. "Do you need help with Jake?"

She needed help with Cole, needed to find a way back to where they'd been. Why couldn't life just have stayed still for a little while?

"No, but you can take Seth to the bathroom and get him changed into pajamas."

"Sure."

"In fact, let's get all the kids into their pajamas before the movie."

"Good idea. Baths tonight or tomorrow?"

"Tomorrow. Gram told me the boys were making mud pies earlier so she already gave them a bath. Faith can skip tonight. I'm hoping they'll fall asleep before the movie is over." As soon as the words left her lips, she saw the night looming large in front of them, and once the kids were in bed it would be just the two of them.

What would they do then? Sensual images immediately came to mind. She sighed. No, they wouldn't be doing that.

"Right. I'll take the older boys and meet you back here."

The evening went better than she anticipated. While *Tinkerbell* flittered across the screen, Cole worked at the kitchen table, a part of the group but separate. The kids lasted longer than she expected, so she was able to say good-night to Cole after they carried the kids upstairs to bed.

She lay awake for a long time thinking about how it had felt to be a family with Cole today. He'd been stilted, but his presence and masculinity were as strong as ever, making her feel safe and very much a woman. How different this weekend would be if his proposal didn't stand between them. It was that picture of what could be that haunted her dreams.

The next morning Dani walked into the kitchen to find Cole had breakfast well under control. They'd decided he would do the early meal and she'd make lunch and each would clean up for the other. Dinner they'd do together.

The kids sat at the island counter, Jake in his high chair near where Cole worked.

"Pancakes," he announced with the first true smile she'd seen all weekend.

Her knees went weak. "Someone woke up on the right side of the bed this morning."

He walked around the island, cupped the back of her head in one hand and kissed her hard. When he lifted his head, he sighed. Satisfaction and relief were in the sound and his relaxed posture.

Behind her, the kids giggled and made kissing sounds.

"Wow." She cleared her throat. "Where did that come from?"

"Sorry." He wandered back around the island and picked up the spatula. "I needed that. Do you want syrup or strawberries?"

"I want an answer."

Cole's gaze swept over the row of little ears gathered around the island. Figuring that was her answer, she sighed. He was right. Wrong time, wrong place.

But he surprised her.

The next thing she knew, he stood beside her, his gaze heated. "I can't be near you and not want you, Dani. So I'm not going to try anymore." His words were a whispered promise in her ear. "I want you in my life. I'm not going to pretend otherwise any longer." He returned to the stove and, with a quick flip of his wrist, turned the pancakes. "I'll give you as much space as I can. So take your time, but I'm not giving up."

Dani slid onto the stool next to Faith. Snagging a strawberry, Dani pretended she wasn't overwhelmed. Gone were the evasions and distance. She was almost disappointed. If he forced the issue, she'd be off the hook.

But no, he was allowing her to work it out for herself.

"Strawberries, please."

The kids played inside and watched cartoons in the morning, but after lunch everyone moved outside. While they kept an eye on the children, Cole used the time to finish the plans for a landscape project. He sat at the patio table while Dani sat reading in a lounger a short distance away.

She wore a light sweater in leaf-green with black jeans, and the autumn air brought a flush to her cheeks. The book in her lap was a mystery by a popular author and obviously funny, because she kept laughing out loud. The happy sound drew his gaze to her lovely profile each time.

"Mommy, push me," Faith called out.

Dani set her book aside and crossed to the swing set. All three of the kids demanded her attention and she gave it freely, pushing one and then the next until all were laughing as they flew through the air.

Cole never tired of watching her, especially with the boys and Faith. She had such patience and love for them and it showed in the little things she did. She had so much to offer, so much love to give; why couldn't she see it?

This morning he'd lost it. Still, he didn't regret kissing her. He wanted to give her time, but contrary to popular opinion he wasn't so laid-back he didn't fight for what he wanted. For Dani he was trying, but he'd needed something to sustain him.

Spending time with her here, in a family situation, was both heaven and hell, a snapshot of what their life together could be—if Dani chose to take a chance rather than give in to fear.

Make no mistake; having no power in how this worked out was killing him. So when his cell rang around two-thirty and he got called to handle a delivery problem at the nursery, he jumped at the chance of escaping for a few minutes.

After closing his laptop, he walked over to tell Dani he'd be leaving for a while.

"Oh." She quickly disguised her disappointment. "Okay."

Pleased by her reaction and the evidence she wanted him there, he changed his mind about leaving. "You know, forget it. My staff can handle it."

"Don't be silly." She shook her head with a half smile. "Go. I can watch the kids on my own for a few hours."

"You shouldn't have to. I committed to being here this weekend." He flipped open his cell to punch in the nursery.

Her fingers wrapped around his, effectively closing the phone. He savored the warmth of her touch.

"Please," she urged him. "Go take care of your business. In fact, why don't you pick—"

She stopped midsentence and went sheet-white. He actively felt her dread and regret and knew she was remembering the last time she'd made such a request, remembering how her husband never returned from the errand.

"Tell me," he whispered, turning his hand so it surrounded her cold one. "What do you want me to bring home?"

"Nothing." She choked out the word. "Never mind." She pulled free, backed away.

"Dani." Her name was a plea.

"I'm fine," she said, but he saw the effort it took her to force a smile. And then her anguish-filled gaze flicked to his. "Come back to me."

CHAPTER TWELVE

DANI TRIED hard not to count the minutes until Cole returned, but she felt every one of those minutes as if they were a year long, especially when she put the kids down for naps and she had no one to distract her.

In her head she knew her fears were exaggerated, not groundless but overblown. Because someone she cared about was out on an errand. It didn't make sense. They'd worked together on the party, each of them running errands, and she hadn't freaked out. But that was before he'd proposed, before they'd spent time together in a family setting.

Before she admitted her love for him.

His arguments against holding on to the guilt and fears of losing Kevin in such a violent act rang through her mind as they had for the past week and a half. Two things struck her—first, that once he left the house, she'd been out of control of what he did and where he went, and second, that she'd never consider blaming Faith for what happened, so was she unreasonable in blaming herself?

She'd been living day to day, providing for Faith but not really looking to the future until Cole made Dani think beyond the walls of her shop and her love for her daughter.

He made her look beyond the moment, made her contemplate a future with more love, more children. The truth was Faith deserved a father. But Dani didn't know if she had the necessary strength to fight her fears and reach for a happy future.

The kids were up and they were playing a game before she started dinner when Cole got home a little before five.

He came in, dropped a bunch of bags on the island, then returned to his truck and came back with more.

"What's all this?" Relieved and overjoyed to see him, she got up to investigate what he'd bought.

"Coffee, diapers, milk, burgers, Chinese food, sub sandwiches, ice cream and a few other items. Basically anything and everything I thought you might have been asking for."

"Cole, you didn't have to do this." Incredibly touched, she peeked in a few bags and found many of the items he mentioned. "Oh, my gosh."

"Yes, I did. I wanted to show you you didn't have to be afraid, that I could pick up a few things and return safe and sound." He emptied the bag of burgers onto the island counter. "Did I get what you wanted?"

"Oh." Overwhelmed, she looked over the varied display of bags. "I was just going to suggest you bring back some flowers." The gaze she shifted to him held an apology. "I know I overreacted—"

"You can't help how you feel. Maybe next time will be easier." He began searching through the bags. "I know it's here somewhere," he muttered. "Ah, here it is." From a brown paper bag he pulled a single red rose. He held the flower out. "For you."

She accepted the rose, beautiful in its simplicity, complex in its message of love. She bent to sniff the lovely scent before lifting shiny eyes to his. "Thank you."

"Can I have fries?" Gabe asked. "And an

egg roll?" Perched on bar stools, the kids began pulling food from the bags.

"I want chicken nuggets," Faith announced. "Are there chicken nuggets?"

Dani bit her lower lip, saddened as the romantic moment evaporated. With a wry grin Cole ran a gentle hand over her hair, but all he said was, "I'll get the plates."

Bath time came after dinner. From the master bath where Faith helped Dani wash baby Jake in the bathtub, she heard shrieks and giggles from the boys' bathroom down the hall.

"They're silly," Faith announced.

"Yes," Dani agreed, careful to keep hold of the slippery baby happily slapping water, "and I bet we can beat them."

Faith nodded eagerly. "Hurry, Mommy, so we can get the best seats for the movie." The best seat meant Alex's extra-large leather recliner. Front and center of the TV, all three kids fit in the chair and felt special when they got to sit in it.

"Wash your face and between your toes, in that order. Then you'll be done. But wait for me to help you get out." Dani lifted Jake from the tub and sat him on a towel. She used a second towel to dry the baby. Next she had Faith stand up and Dani lifted her out and set her beside Jake.

Catching a glimpse of color out of the corner of her eye made Dani glance at the single red rose in a vase on the vanity. That made seven. Besides the one Cole had handed to her, she'd found one in the hall, the kitchen, Jake's room and on her bedside table. She didn't know how he was doing it. He'd been everywhere yet he never seemed to be gone.

Seriously, a Navy SEAL had nothing on Cole Sullivan's stealth skills. Or his romantic ones.

Every time she came across a new rose, she heard his voice in her head saying, *I love you.*

And each time, the words sounded more real, more right.

"Mommy! I'm all dry." Faith's tousled head popped out of the top of the towel wrapped around her. "My hair isn't wet." She protested, blowing at the hair hanging in her eyes.

Oops. Dani focused on her disgruntled

daughter then quickly checked on Jake and found him crawling naked into the bedroom.

"Sorry, Sweat Pea." She released Faith to grab the escaping baby, making him giggle by tickling his bare tummy. For good measure Dani tickled Faith's bare little tummy, too, earning more laughter. "Okay. Let's get jammies on the two of you and then we can go down for the movie."

"Yeah." Faith ran to her suitcase. "I'm going to stay awake for the whole movie. Gabe says Transformers are cool."

They beat the guys. And Dani found another red rose in the family room on the end table next to the couch where she usually sat. How was he doing that? And where was his stash?

Gabe and Seth came running into the room and headed straight for the entertainment center. They got the movie going and hopped into the chair with Faith. Dani teased them about stealing her seat, but they weren't budging.

Cole sauntered into the room and his eyes went straight to her and the message in them was the same as that of the roses, the love he felt there for her to see. Holding her gaze, he deliberately slid into the corner of the couch where she usually sat and patted the seat next to him.

"The movie is starting," he said. "This is the current release, you don't want to miss any. Transformers are cool."

"Start without me. I'm going to grab a soda." Being a complete coward, she escaped to the kitchen. Where she found another rose. This one in the refrigerator. It made her smile and gave her enough courage to join him on the couch when she returned to the family room.

Okay, there was no snuggling. She wasn't ready for that, especially in front of the children. But Dani began to accept that Cole wasn't going to give up. Surprisingly, instead of feeling crowded, his passive but romantic campaign was working.

She just might give him the chance he wanted, once this weekend was behind her and she had time to think things through in a less hectic atmosphere.

The sickening sense of dread spilling through her when she'd nearly asked Cole to bring flowers home had been a shock. The ridiculous fear an ugly reminder of what she'd allowed her life to come to. She didn't want that for herself. And she really didn't want that for Faith.

Dani knew if she continued to let trepidation rule her, eventually it would bleed over onto Faith.

So she didn't snuggle, but she relaxed next to Cole, laughing and cheering with him as the Transformers kicked alien butt.

Halfway through the movie she found rose number ten in the downstairs bathroom. That had to be the last of them, there were no more rooms left!

"Romantic nut," she muttered when she reclaimed her spot next to him. "They're lovely. Thank you."

He ran his hand down the back of her head. "I wanted you to know life may be fragile, but it can also be beautiful."

Pumped up on the action, the kids made it through the whole movie, and then it was time for bed.

Dani stopped on the way to the master suite to tuck the boys in and give them kisses goodnight. Of course she discovered another rose.

"That's from Uncle Cole," Gabe told her. "It's a surprise for you."

"It certainly is." She swept the dark hair off Gabe's forehead and gave him a kiss. "He's been surprising me all night."

"He likes you." Seth giggled in his bed three feet away.

"I like him, too," Dani admitted as she gave Seth his kiss.

"Are you going to give him a good-night kiss, too?" Gabe wanted to know.

"Yeah," Cole said from the doorway. "Do I get a good-night kiss, too?"

"You sure do. From Faith." Dani picked up Faith and walked toward Cole. "Say good-night."

"'Night, Cole." Faith threw her little arms around Cole's neck and gave him a huge kiss on the cheek. "I love you."

Cole gave her a squeeze as he met Dani's gaze over Faith's head. "I love you, too."

Her heart melted. Oh, he cheated, using his affection for her daughter to get to her.

"Well, good night."

She moved to slide by him, but he caught her waist and pulled her close for a quick kiss. "Sleep tight."

Holding Faith to her like a shield, she escaped down the hall to the master bedroom.

Turned out Transformers were a little scary for a three-year-old. Dani expected Faith to demand she sleep in the boys' room with Gabe and Seth, but the movie had spooked her and she wanted to sleep with her mom.

Distracted by the kiss, Dani went to the left side of the bed to tuck Faith in and that's when she saw the rose. The covers had been turned down and a single red rose rested on the pristine white cover of the pillow.

Right, passive as a battleship.

She sighed. She might just have to marry the man.

Faith squirmed up close to Dani when she switched off the bedside lamp. Light cast a silvery glow over the gray carpet through the half-open bedroom door, keeping the room from total darkness. She'd left the door ajar so she could listen for the boys and the baby.

"Can we have the light on, Mommy?"

"Little scaredy-cat. There's enough light from the hall. And I won't let anything happen to you."

"Do you think Cole could beat up the mean bots?"

"I do." Dani cuddled Faith close, resting her cheek against her baby's soft curls. Bad parent, Dani chastised herself for not noticing the movie was upsetting her daughter. "I'm sorry the movie scared you."

"It didn't scare me," Faith denied, "I liked the Transformers. But I didn't like the mean bots."

The pounding of little feet preceded Seth and Gabe into the room. Dani sat up as the boys reached the side of the bed.

"There's a noise in our room," Gabe said.

"It's a mean bot," Seth informed her.

"It's not a mean bot," Gabe sharply corrected his brother. "It was just a noise." But he looked hopefully up at Dani. "Can we sleep with you?"

Seth scowled at Gabe and then climbed onto the bed. "Mean bot," he insisted.

"Mommy—"

"I'm sure Gabe is right." Dani cut off the question, lifting the blankets so Gabe could scramble up and into the bed. "There are no mean bots in the house." She ruffled Gabe's hair. "I thought you boys had seen this movie before."

He nodded. "We did. Transformers are cool. But after the movie, Seth slept with Mama and Daddy."

Right. Dani guessed Gabe had, too.

"What's going on in here?" Cole appeared in the open doorway. He wore sweatpants but no shirt and looked strong and fit, backlit by the hall light. Well up to fighting off menacing alien bots. "You guys having a party?"

"Uncle Cole!"

"There are mean bots in our room."

"Can you beat up the mean bots?"

The kids all talked at once, but he quickly caught on to the problem. His rueful gaze met Dani's. "We should have stuck with *Tinkerbell*."

She nodded.

"I'll go check out the boys' room, make sure there are no mean bots hanging out."

"And beat them up," Faith called.

"Yep. If I find any, they're getting beaten down." Cole winked at Dani and disappeared.

When he returned a few minutes later, he carried Jake with him. "No mean bots, but I found a baby awake and standing in his crib."

"Is he okay?" Dani asked.

"Yeah, probably just disturbed by all the activity."

"He can sleep with us," Faith offered.

"Yeah, Uncle Cole, come sleep with us."

Sitting up against the headboard, Dani patted the pillows in invitation. "You may as well join the party. I don't think anyone is going to get much sleep tonight."

"Don't mind if I do." He sauntered across the room and climbed in on the far side. He propped himself up on one elbow facing her. His eyes devoured her, making her feel beautiful without a shred of makeup.

Jake crawled into the middle of the bed, stopped to survey everyone watching him and then crawled over and squeezed in between his brothers.

Dani pulled the blanket up around his shoulders, making sure all the kids were warm and comfortable. She glanced at Cole and then away again.

"I'm sorry," she whispered, and nodded at the crowded bed. "I should have known the movie was too much for them. Faith doesn't usually watch action films—"

"Stop beating yourself up, Dani. You're a great mother. This is all an adventure for them. And I'm right where I want to be."

Her heart melted. Because she knew that was true. He'd made his feelings clear. She'd been the one to hesitate, the one who didn't know her own feelings.

His fingers tangled with hers on the pillow above the kids' heads. Contrary to her prediction, they had already settled down and were asleep or close to it.

"This is what I want with you, Dani. A bed filled with the love we've made. I want to grow things with you in the garden and sit with you on the deck watching sunsets and grandchildren."

The picture he painted sounded heavenly. She could actually see a future—a brother and sister for Faith, working with Cole getting their hands dirty in the garden, holding hands as they watched grandkids frolic.

She curled her fingers around his. "Yes."

"Yes?" His hand tightened.

"Yes, you're where I want you to be. Yes, I want to have children with you. Yes, let's build things and watch sunsets together. Yes, I love you."

Slowly his smile grew, becoming a sexy grin. He leaned over the kids and she met him in a soft kiss that was way too short.

"Mommy, is Cole going to be my daddy?" Faith's sleepy voice asked.

Love rushed through her, warming Dani and opening her heart to the hope of the future. She felt love for her daughter and love for the man who had brought light back to her life.

"That's right, baby." Dani caressed him with her eyes. "Mommy's going to marry Cole."

On sale from 17th September 2010
Don't miss out!

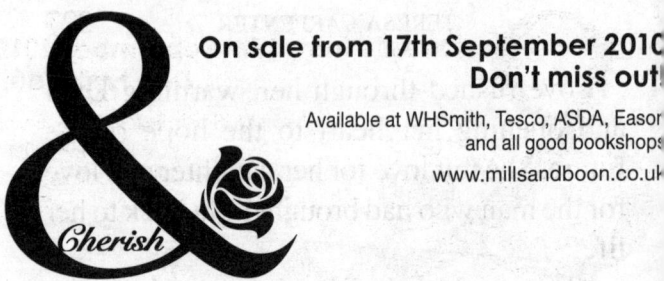

Available at WHSmith, Tesco, ASDA, Eason and all good bookshops

www.millsandboon.co.uk

Cherish

TEXAS CINDERELLA *by Victoria Pade*

A hidden diamond and a dramatic feud! Will Tate be able to keep his family secrets from sassy journalist Tanya, even as he falls in love?

THE TEXAS CEO'S SECRET *by Nicole Foster*

Katerina and Blake were meant to be friends, linked by marriage – but not to each other. But a passionate kiss changes everything.

STAR-CROSSED SWEETHEARTS *by Jackie Braun*

Hiding from the press in Italy, actress Atlanta wants to be alone. Will former bad boy Angelo show her that the limelight is fleeting and it's family and love that count?

SECRET PRINCE, INSTANT DADDY! *by Raye Morgan*

When pretty Ayme tracks him down, deposed royal Darius, sure he is the father of her late sister's baby, must decide how he can fulfil his destiny and find his own happiness.

AT HOME IN STONE CREEK *by Linda Lael Miller*

Everyone in Ashley's life is marrying and starting families. Now Jack, the man who broke her heart years ago, is back. But is he who she thinks he is?

Cherish

On sale from 17th September 2010
Don't miss out!

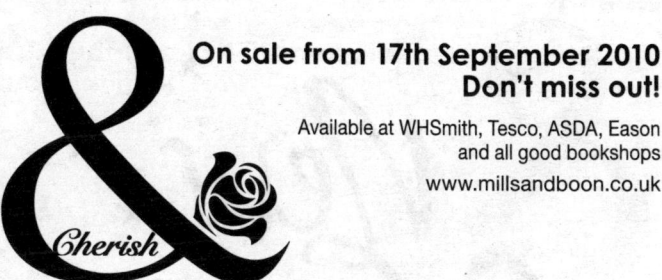

Available at WHSmith, Tesco, ASDA, Eason and all good bookshops

www.millsandboon.co.uk

Cherish

A MIRACLE FOR HIS SECRET SON
by Barbara Hannay

Freya never intended Gus to find out about their son. But when young Nick needs a kidney transplant she tracks him down. Could this be their chance to be a family?

PROUD RANCHER, PRECIOUS BUNDLE
by Donna Alwood

Wyatt and Elli have already had a run-in. But when a baby is left on his doorstep, Wyatt needs help. Will romance between them flare as they care for baby Darcy?

ACCIDENTALLY PREGNANT!
by Rebecca Winters

Left pregnant and alone, Irena is determined to keep her baby a secret. Can Vincenzo, the man she had a passionate affair with, give her the love she needs?

Cherish

New Voices

Do you dream of being a romance writer?

Mills & Boon are looking for fresh writing talent in our biggest ever search!

And this time…our readers have a say in who wins!

For information on how to enter or get involved go to

www.romanceisnotdead.com

INTRODUCED BY BESTSELLING AUTHOR KATIE FFORDE

Four fabulous new writers

Lynn Raye Harris
Kept for the Sheikh's Pleasure

Nikki Logan
Seven-Day Love Story

Molly Evans
Her No.1 Doctor

Ann Lethbridge
The Governess and the Earl

We know you're going to love them!

Available 20th August 2010

www.millsandboon.co.uk

Bestselling author
PENNY JORDAN
presents
The Parenti Dynasty

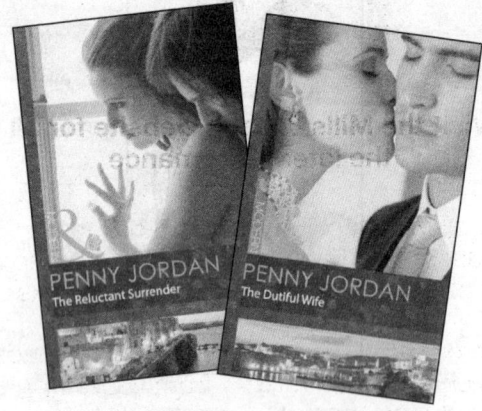

*Power, privilege and passion
The worlds of big business and royalty unite…*

The epic romance of Saul and Giselle begins with…

THE RELUCTANT SURRENDER
On sale October 2010

and concludes with

THE DUTIFUL WIFE
On sale November 2010

Don't miss it!

Discover Pure Reading Pleasure with

MILLS & BOON

Visit the Mills & Boon website for all the latest in romance

- **Buy** all the latest releases, backlist and eBooks

- **Join** our community and chat to authors and other readers

- **Win** with our fantastic online competitions

- **Tell us** what you think by signing up to our reader panel

- **Find out** more about our authors and their books

- **Free** online reads from your favourite authors

- **Sign** up for our free monthly eNewsletter

- **Rate** and review books with our star system

www.millsandboon.co.uk

Follow us at twitter.com/millsandboonuk

Become a fan at facebook.com/romancehq

0910_N0ZED

2 FREE BOOKS
AND A SURPRISE GIFT

We would like to take this opportunity to thank you for reading this Mills & Boon® book by offering you the chance to take TWO more specially selected books from the Romance series absolutely FREE! We're also making this offer to introduce you to the benefits of the Mills & Boon® Book Club™—

- **FREE** home delivery
- **FREE** gifts and competitions
- **FREE** monthly Newsletter
- **Exclusive Mills & Boon Book Club offers**
- **Books available before they're in the shops**

Accepting these FREE books and gift places you under no obligation to buy, you may cancel at any time, even after receiving your free shipment. Simply complete your details below and return the entire page to the address below. You don't even need a stamp!

YES Please send me 2 free Romance books and a surprise gift. I understand that unless you hear from me, I will receive 5 superb new stories every month including two 2-in-1 books priced at £4.99 each and a single book priced at £3.19, postage and packing free. I am under no obligation to purchase any books and may cancel my subscription at any time. The free books and gift will be mine to keep in any case.

Ms/Mrs/Miss/Mr _____ Initials _____

Surname _____
Address _____
_____
_____ Postcode _____
E-mail _____

Send this whole page to: Mills & Boon Book Club, Free Book Offer, FREEPOST NAT 10298, Richmond, TW9 1BR

Offer valid in UK only and is not available to current Mills & Boon Book Club subscribers to this series. Overseas and Eire please write for details.. We reserve the right to refuse an application and applicants must be aged 18 years or over. Only one application per household. Terms and prices subject to change without notice. Offer expires 30th November 2010. As a result of this application, you may receive offers from Harlequin Mills & Boon and other carefully selected companies. If you would prefer not to share in this opportunity please write to The Data Manager, PO Box 676, Richmond, TW9 1WU.

Mills & Boon® is a registered trademark owned by Harlequin Mills & Boon Limited.
The Mills & Boon® Book Club™ is being used as a trademark.